THE CORONER HAD NO COMMENT

M. J. VAN BUREN

KAW VALLEY SPRING

Copyright © 2023 Marjorie J. Van Buren

All rights reserved

This is a work of fiction. All names, characters, places, organizations, and events portrayed in this book are products of the author's imagination or are used fictitiously. Any similarity to real persons, living or dead, is coincidental and not intended by the author.

No part of this book may be reproduced, or stored in a retrieval system, or transmitted in any form or by any means, electronic, mechanical, photocopying, recording, or otherwise, without express written permission of the publisher.

ISBN: 9781736705032

Cover design by: Samuel Milord
Printed in the United States of America

For Lynn, always

AUTHOR'S COMMENTS

Warning to any and all: if you think you recognize someone in this book--yourself, a friend, a distant acquaintance--you're wrong! This is not a roman a clef.

Apologies to the late, much-lamented Topeka Natural Food Co-op for my misuse of its general configuration as it might have appeared in the '70s. If the co-op had its share of characters, none of those appear in my book, and I'm quite sure none of them were ever murdered!

Apologies to coroners and medical examiners anywhere, but especially in Topeka and in Kansas generally. I'm sure all are more conscientious than those described here.

As most fiction writers do, I've taken liberties with the setting--streets, buildings, highways. I've also played fast and loose with certain government institutions, the ways they interacted, and especially the way records were handled back in the early days of computerization.

In fact, to be blunt, folks, this is a work of fiction. All names, characters, places, businesses, organizations, events and incidents are either products of my imagination or are used fictitiously. Any similarity to real persons, living or dead, or to actual events, is purely coincidental and not intended by the author.

CHAPTER 1

Of course the turtle hadn't been frozen in the beginning. At first, the turtle had been merely dead. Maggie had made out that much between the sobs. "Can you come down right now, right away?" Sondra had said on the phone, her voice soft but very intense. "I know it's late, but I've just gotten home and I've lost my daughters and I've run over Yertle and I'm sure he's dead and I don't think I can handle it alone."

The call had come around midnight, long after Maggie's usual 10:30 bedtime, and the ringing phone had shaken her like a slap. "Well, she was asleep, Sondra," she'd heard Mike say softly, "but I think she's awake now!" Mike had stretched the cord across to hand Maggie the phone, shaking his head with a skeptical look in his dark eyes. He tended to react that way to Sondra, even at more reasonable hours.

But Sondra had sounded so desperate Maggie couldn't bring herself to demur. "I'll be there in just a moment," she'd promised before hanging up the phone. "Besides," she explained to Mike, who was watching her from the bed, "I'm awake now. If I don't go, I'll just lie here wondering." As she spoke, she stood up and slipped out of a light blue chemise. After pulling on a bright pink cotton sweater and running her fingers distractedly through her long dark brown curls a couple of times, she tugged a pair of drawstring denim pants over what she thought of as her Earth Mother hips.

"I don't know how long I'll be. Probably not very, but don't wait up. You have to go to work in the morning." She balanced against the padded edge of the waterbed to slip on first one cork-soled Birkenstock sandal and then its mate. Yawning and shaking her head, she stepped around the end of the bed to Mike's side. "See you later," she murmured, bending down to brush his lips with her own.

"Okay, Tiger, don't stay too long. You have to go to work too, you know," said Mike, picking up his book again.

Maggie felt her way in the dark down the carpeted stairs to the front door of the modest split-level house that was home to her husband, two children, and herself. Grabbing a knitted shawl from the hook by the front door and flipping the outside light switch with the same practiced motion, she opened the door with the other hand and slipped out into the crisp suburban night.

Keys? No. She went back inside, located the Guatemalan-woven canvas bag that served her as a purse and emergency shopping bag, and fumbled briefly for her keys. Stuffing the handful of keys in her pants pocket, she again went outside, snapping the lock automatically before she shut the door.

Beyond the circles of light from the small lamp over the door and the street light on the corner, the night was dark and still. Stars glittered in a moonless sky. Maggie stepped briskly down the sidewalk, keeping one hand in her pocket on the key ring with its attached police whistle, and looking around in what she hoped was a confident, no-nonsense manner.

Sondra's house was only a short block away, and the neighborhood was a low-crime area, its comfortable ten to fifteen-year-old frame and brick homes well-spaced on grassy lawns amid oaks, maples, and elms. But even in this friendly area there were lots of shadows. Maggie was aware again of how much she hated feeling afraid as a woman walking alone after dark, and she puzzled for a moment over whether if she could change her attitude—no longer *feel* afraid—would that then mean that she wouldn't *need* to be afraid? Could Danger smell fear, like a dog or a horse? Maggie shook her head again, this time to shake away the fear and the philosophizing and focus on

Sondra's needs.

She had known Sondra for about two years, though she'd heard of her earlier without the name meaning anything at the time. It had been a curious snatch of a story, overheard in Laurie's kitchen one Tuesday night. Laurie and Suz were discussing some people they obviously both knew, speculating about "how Sondra puts up with it, and what Nora thinks she is doing."

"She's always talking about it being a matter of spiritual growth and personal freedom. Of course, I think a woman has to be free," Laurie had said.

"But a *menage a trois* is always pretty difficult to handle. And somebody is likely to end up getting hurt," Suz observed, pouring boiling water over three bags of Red Zinger in the tea pot.

"And as usual, the man is the one who gets the best of both. In this case, he gets two women and his wife can't even complain that he's sneaking around on her because he isn't!" Laurie pronounced with a finality that buried the point of the paring knife in the cutting board and sent a piece of the apple she had been slicing skittering off into the corner of the kitchen.

Maggie had actually met Sondra months later at The General Store, Topeka's health food cooperative and unofficial gathering place for the city's "alternative community." Maggie was doing her volunteer turn as cashier one spring Saturday when a slender, blonde thirty-something woman in a brightly-flowered skirt hurried into the store and looked around with an air that suggested a hungry but absent-minded squirrel trying to find last year's cache.

"Hello, Sondra," a tall thin man in a Co-op America t-shirt had called out from behind the rack of organic blue corn chips.

"Oh, hi, Leslie," the woman had responded distractedly. "Is there an order of pancake flour here for me?" she continued, addressing her question to the room in general.

When no one else seemed to be going to answer, Maggie cleared her throat tentatively. "Um, I'm Maggie Tenwhistle. Can I help you?"

The woman whirled in Maggie's direction, her gathered skirt billowing gracefully as she turned. "I need to find my pancake flour. I've got maybe twenty people coming for pancakes and tofu-eggs, and I have the smoked tofu, but they were supposed to have ordered the pancake flour for me special and if it isn't here, I don't know what I'll do, because if I have to buy it at the supermarket, then what will I do with the order when it does come in—I could never use up that much pancake flour by myself."

The woman paused to breathe. A bit breathless herself, Maggie stared at her. Then, recollecting her best business manner, she smiled and said, "What is your name, please? And I'll go look in the cool room for your order."

"Oh," said the woman. "I'm Sondra Sampson. And your name was....?"

"Maggie Tenwhistle," replied Maggie, already on her way back to the cool storage vault. "It's nice to meet you."

As it turned out, the order was on the shelf, just where it should have been, and before she left, Sondra invited Maggie to the neighborhood equinox celebration she was holding in her backyard that evening. "Come for the meal if you like, or come just for the ritual, or whatever. It's very informal. And bring your family."

Maggie couldn't imagine Mike or either of her teenaged children being very much interested in smoked tofu eggs, but she had been curious enough about the woman to go to the celebration herself. She and Sondra had been more or less friends ever since.

By now Maggie had reached Sondra's door. She opened the wrought-iron-decorated storm door and knocked briskly on the inner panel. She listened briefly and then opened the door just a crack. "Sondra? It's Maggie! Sondra?"

In a moment, she heard Sondra call out from upstairs.

"Come on in. I'm up here. Will you just come on up?"

Her voice sounded as it had on the phone, soft and intense, but lacking its usual exuberance. As though she were in a trance, or in shock, Maggie thought, with a pang of concern. "I'm coming," she said, and quickly climbed the stairs to Sondra's loft-bedroom. There she found her friend sitting cross-legged on the bed, the turtle in front of her. Her eyes were red and her face tear-stained.

Maggie stopped at the edge of the bed. "Are you okay?" she asked tentatively.

"Look at him," Sondra pleaded. "Do you think he is really dead?"

Maggie looked at the turtle. The brown and orange shell was crushed, and one leg hung unmoving from the lip of what had been its protective home. Yes, of course it's dead, silly, she thought. How could anyone possibly think otherwise? But Sondra was serious, so Maggie merely said, "Yes, I think he's really dead," keeping her voice as steady as possible.

"I think so, too," Sondra said slowly. "He was down at the edge of the driveway when I got home. I didn't see him at all. I just heard the crunch."

She isn't meaning to be funny—it isn't funny, it's sad, Maggie told herself sternly. She sat down on the edge of the bed, carefully so as not to disturb the body. Keep a straight face, change the subject, that's the ticket, she thought, as a giggle threatened to force itself past her firmly-pressed lips. "You said something about your kids. I knew they were due to spend some time with their dad?"

"They left today to go with him to Albuquerque. They didn't want to go. I had to promise them all kinds of things to get them on the plane."

"I'm sure once they get there, they'll be fine," Maggie said soothingly, putting an arm around Sondra. "It's good for them to go now, while they can. It gets harder later on."

"But I miss them so terribly already. I didn't think I would. And now I've run over Yertle." She turned into Maggie's comforting arm, and sniffled quietly on her shoulder for a long moment before raising her head and turning back to the turtle. "I feel so guilty. I never should have left him out."

"When will the girls be back with you?" Maggie asked.

"They are going to be gone for two months. Sam's on a dig, and they won't be back till the middle of May. He is really dead, isn't he? He's starting to get cold." Sondra was stroking the turtle.

Maggie thought turtles were cold to begin with, but she reached out to touch the cracked shell, trying not to show the ripple of something like revulsion that she felt. "Yes, I think he's pretty cold," she agreed. "Maybe you should consider moving him off your bed."

"Oh, no, I wouldn't do that!" Sondra turned to look at Maggie with a frown. "I'll keep him here tonight. He shouldn't be alone. I'll keep a vigil."

"Oh." Maggie couldn't think of anything else to say. She knew Sondra had strong beliefs about the movement of souls through the realms of the dead, but she hadn't realized they extended to reptiles.

"I think I'm going to be fine now," Sondra was saying. "Thank you so very much for coming down. I don't think I could have made it without you."

"So I gave her another hug and left her there, sitting on the bed with that turtle," Maggie told her husband over the breakfast table next morning. "I expect she sat up with it all night. I hope I hear from her today. But I dasn't try to call her, in case she's sleeping. At least not until this evening."

"Pretty strange, if you ask me," Mike said, buttering his third piece of toast."

The sun streaming in the window of the dining nook settled warmly on the oiled oak table and glowed in Maggie's glass of cranapple juice. "Well, think how dull life would be if we were all alike," Maggie said, as she spooned up the last of the corn flakes from her bowl. "I'm sure other people would think we were pretty strange, too."

"Are we going to be able to have lunch together?" Mike asked, scraping his chair back on the gray-blue vinyl flooring.

Maggie cringed, but didn't mention the marks she had spent so much time trying to rub out the week before. "So far as I know now, lunch is on," she replied. "I should be able to go at noon, unless someone has an emergency. You could call me when you know for sure what your schedule is."

"Okay, or you call me if I forget." Mike was finishing his last sip of coffee. "I'll see you later, then."

He slipped on his suit coat and started for the door.

"Hey, you!" Maggie stood up and pursed her lips, making a smacking sound. Mike turned around and came back to meet her for a decidedly possessive hug and a quick but unequivocal kiss. "See what I mean about us being strange? Here we are, married nearly twenty years and still making lunch dates and kissing whenever we leave the house. That sounds pretty strange to me!"

"Um-hm, see you, Tiger," said Mike, and he was out the door.

Alone amid the ruins of breakfast, Maggie stacked her cereal bowl and Mike's toast plate on top of the plate Geoff had left in the sink, coated with cheese and picante sauce from his standard morning quesadilla. Glancing at the clock on the microwave, she did a quick calculation. Time enough to start a load of wash if she hurried. Grabbing the towels and dish cloth from over the sink, she headed for the laundry room adjacent to the kitchen. Upstairs in the bathroom a moment later, she gathered up a load of brown and pink towels, most of them from the floor. Would Geoff ever learn to hang up his wet towels, she wondered? Perhaps. His sister Alyssa, a freshman in college, seemed to have developed the art at Bethany last semester. There was still hope.

The washer was soon churgling away. Back upstairs again,

Maggie brushed her shoulder-length hair as smooth as it would go. Checking her watch, she estimated she had eighteen minutes to get to the office. Not that any of the three financial planners who were her bosses would know—or care—if she was a little late, but she tried not to take advantage of their laid-back style except in extremity. She checked her dark blue-green skirt and neatly-tucked aqua knit blouse in the bedroom mirror, and flicked the quartz-crystal-and-turquoise-earrings that dangled from her ears. Mike preferred the mini-skirts she'd worn a while back, but she thought the mid-calf length not only looked more serious but felt elegant and feminine as well.

Down the stairs again. (Having once kept count of the number of trips she made up and down in a day, Maggie considered it one of her goals in life to retire to a one-story house.) Down the stairs, handbag and shawl, throw the lock, and out the door. Her middle-aged bronze Datsun coupe sat in the driveway in front of the light green frame house Maggie and her family had lived in for nearly five years.

As she strode toward the car, she reached into the red, yellow, and blue striped bag for her keys. When she didn't come up with them immediately, she shook the bag sharply, listening for the reassuring jangle that said the keys were there all right, just buried under comb, checkbook, pens, note pad, and old credit card receipts.

No jangle. Now what? Maggie began to dig anxiously through the clutter, peering into the depths of the bag that suddenly seemed like hostile territory. Last night! Of course. She'd taken her keys when she went to Sondra's, and what had she done with them when she came home?

Okay, the first step is to get back into the house, she told herself. She tossed her bag on top of the car and dug the extra house key from under the plastic mulch around the roses that edged the carport. Inside, she quickly located the missing key ring on her bedside table. A check of the time showed she now had fourteen minutes to get to work. Not quite enough, but, oh, well! She re-locked the door, tucked the extra key back in its hiding place, and hurried out to the car.

CHAPTER 2

Usually Maggie enjoyed her drive downtown. Since she didn't have to be at work until eight-thirty, she routinely avoided the heavy morning rush of State government workers like Mike, who had to be on duty in the central offices of the Kansas Bureau of Investigation by eight. (Not that Topeka traffic was ever really bad by big city standards.) She looked forward to the time in the car as a chance to shift gears, morning and evening, from home mode to work mode and back again. Now, however, pulling smoothly into the stream of downtown-bound traffic on the interstate bypass, her thoughts returned to Sondra. Should Maggie have called this morning? No, Sondra would probably be asleep, worn out with grief over that darned turtle and worry over her daughters off to New Mexico with their archeologist father. If only Sondra could....

"No," Maggie told herself sternly, "there is nothing you can do about Sondra's problems. She has to solve them herself. And you need to get into workday gear."

When she'd first left the district court for this job as secretary to Blain, Towneshend, and Hannigan, it had felt like something of a let-down, even though the money was better. Working for the Clerk of the District Court at the county courthouse, she'd supervised ten junior clerks and been responsible for cases involving millions of dollars. At BTH, she was the only hired help, and for the first few weeks even though she was always busy, she felt as though she weren't really working. Finally she realized what was making her uneasy was only the absence of the familiar pressure of too-much-to-do-

and-never-enough-time-to-do-it. Now, after six months on the new job, she could thankfully say she'd never made a better move.

"It's like the old joke about banging your head against the wall because it feels so good when you quit!" Maggie'd told her Tuesday night group recently. "Except in my case, it took me a while to realize that what I was missing was the pain!"

Traffic was flowing smoothly around downtown, and Maggie arrived at the fifth floor office of BTH only a few minutes late. Even so, the phone was ringing as she unlocked the door. It was one of Constance Blain's clients, and Maggie was able to answer a question about the sales charge on a mutual fund Constance had recommended. "I'd be happy to have her call you, Mrs. Greene," Maggie said. "I'm expecting her any minute," she added wickedly, knowing Constance hated handling any calls before 10:00 or 10:30. "All right, I'll tell her you called." She tore off the phone note and slipped it into the clip on the front of her desk.

The small suite of offices occupied by Blain, Towneshend, and Hannigan was in the southwest corner of an 1890's building that had originally been a bank. In the reception area, Maggie's desk was overhung by a large glass chandelier, one of the few original fixtures, long since converted to electricity from gas. A couple of functional but not lavish arm chairs, upholstered in blue velveteen, stood on either side of a small table near the entrance. File cabinets lined one wall and shelves the opposite, while Maggie's workspace sprawled between. Her Selectric typewriter and the office fax were conveniently located to one side of her desk. The copy machine was not-so-conveniently located in a small alcove next to Constance Blaine's office.

As the senior broker in the group, Constance had the corner office. Tall windows, sparkling in the morning sun, looked over smaller buildings toward the state Capitol and the historic Jayhawk Hotel, now a high-rent office building. Under the windows, on a credenza of warm cherry wood, two gray stone owls bookended Stocktrader's Almanac, Moody's,

Standard and Poor's Guide and a few other reference works.

One corner of Constance's desk held a cluster of family photos—nieces, nephews, and children of friends, so far as Maggie had been able to ascertain. A couple of neat piles of reading material and a gray stone jar that matched the bookends were the only other objects on the large desk.

When Constance arrived unsmiling and monosyllabic at around 9:00 a.m., her first concern would be coffee, strong and black. So Maggie started it right away, sniffing appreciatively as she measured the rich, dark grounds into the filter. If only coffee ever tasted as good as it smelled!

Constance's second requirement, after the coffee was in her tall blue and gold mug, would be the office copy of *The Wall Street Journal*, which Maggie had picked up from the front hall, across from the quaint operator-operated elevator which was one of the old building's charming features. Thus fortified, Constance would retire to her corner for at least an hour, venturing forth only to refill the mug.

Red-haired Terence Hannigan, the youngest of Maggie's three bosses, had the small office nearest the coffee machine, the refrigerator, and the water cooler. It was also the part of the suite that contained an old vault, left over from the days when each business needed its own fireproof record storage on the premises. The vault, with its highly decorated red and gold door perpetually propped open, was now mere storage space, with shelves containing only inactive files, boxes of holiday decorations, and extra coffee filters.

The window ledges in Terence's space were cluttered with autographed theater programs, snapshots of foreign cityscapes, and other memorabilia of his cultural adventures. Terence would arrive around 9:15, full of enthusiasm and eager to share some anecdote he'd heard on NPR coming in, or, since this was Monday, ready to regale Maggie with stories of his weekend's social activities. Terence was a gourmet cook and a dancer, with a dancer's lithe, muscular body, and Maggie gathered he was much in demand as an escort among the hip young single women of Topeka.

To hear him talk, he was also a connoisseur of fine wines, though Maggie supposed she would never be in a position to check on that, either. Mike, contending that they couldn't afford expensive wines as a routine matter, stoutly refused to try one even for a special occasion—lest it prove worth the price. "I'd rather not know what I'm missing," he would say stubbornly whenever Maggie suggested trying a bottle of a "saucy little valpolicella" or an "aromatic French chablis of exceptional quality" she'd heard Terence praise. Sometimes she wished Mike were just a little bit less practical. But he was a Taurus, and was as hard to budge as any of his sign.

Other than an attentive ear for his stories, Terence's main requirements of his secretary centered around keeping his client files orderly, his desk presentable, and his calendar clear on Friday afternoons. Nelson Towneshend, by contrast, was all organization and business and needed no one to pick up after him. His office, with the big bay windows Maggie loved, was always meticulously kept. Several large framed prints by contemporary artists added a touch of color, but did little to alleviate a certain starkly impersonal atmosphere. Nelson relied heavily on Maggie to supply the personal touch with clients. Her friendly Midwestern voice on the phone was welcomed by many who respected Nelson's gifts as a stock picker but found his clipped British accent and formal manner too austere. As the clients got acquainted with Maggie and she learned more about the business, she was finding herself more frequently relaying questions and answers between her employer and the people who paid for his advice.

Actually, Nelson was not English, but a native of Nigeria, a rather small man with a round face and gleaming dark-chocolate skin. Though his manner might seem cold to some, Maggie found him easy to work for. He was decisive, calm, and fair, and he had never asked her to lie to a caller. And based on what his clients were earning on their money, she'd told Mike recently, Nelson was surely whom she would seek to emulate in professional expertise, someday when she got her own securities license. Nelson would arrive last, not much before 10:00, and would begin his day at the Quotron machine, checking price trends on the major exchanges, before studying the *Journal* when Constance finished with it or pursuing some abstruse research of his own.

By the time Constance arrived on this morning, the smell of fresh-brewed coffee had percolated through the suite, and Maggie was hard at work revising a letter formulated for some of Terence's best clients. Her proofreading and editing skills had been near-legendary at the district court, and her present employers made good use of them as well. The rest of the morning flew by, with just time for entering some information on the database and running off a hypothetical on Templeton World Fund for Nelson before Mike called to claim his lunch date.

Lunch was a quick outing to the Pocket Corner, a pita-bread sandwich shop near Maggie's office. "The Director has a new brainstorm, something about computerizing coroners' reports," Mike apologized as they stood in line to order. "So I have a one o'clock appointment with someone at the Judicial Administrator's Office.

"One ham-and-cream cheese, no mustard; one Veggie Combo, extra cheese; an ice tea; and a water with no ice," he responded to the busy counter-woman's query.

"And these desserts," Maggie added quickly, holding up two small packets wrapped in waxed paper.

"Shall I drop you off, or do you want to walk?" Mike asked Maggie a few minutes later, as he polished off the last of a piece of rich carrot cake with creamy icing.

"Oh, I'll walk, I guess. It's a pretty day." And it was. The sky was a clear blue, with just enough white clouds for contrast. The sun, which only a few weeks earlier had been weak and low in the sky, shone warmly on Maggie's face. She smiled as she walked briskly up the hill toward the hundred-year-old Fountain Building that housed Blain, Towneshend, and Hannigan as well as several other brokers and financial services offices, a lawyer or two, and a holistic health care center.

The building glowed red-brown in the sunlight. The huge rough stone blocks that formed the base of the facade contrasted with the elaborate carving above. Until she went to work in the Fountain Building, Maggie has supposed the rock facade to be sandstone. But Terence had informed her it was native Kansas limestone, painted (for some unaccountable reason) a sandstone red. Since watching workmen touch up the paint only a few months earlier, Maggie now knew Terence had not been pulling her leg.

Arriving at the front doors, Maggie paused with a hand on a gleaming brass doorknob and looked once more at the glorious spring sky. With another smile and a soft sigh, she turned to enter, leaning back slightly to balance against the weight of the heavy oak door.

In the office, Maggie found Constance and Terence standing beside her desk in a loud discussion of the probable impact of the latest Middle East crisis on the future of international petroleum prices. "OPEC doesn't dare let things get out of hand," Terence was saying. "If prices get too high"—he illustrated with a dramatic sweep of his hand—"even the United States will start taking energy conservation and alternate fuels development seriously. And they can't afford to let that happen." He gestured again, indicating the direction of oil prices in that eventuality.

"You're right that it's a balancing act," Constance agreed as she grabbed for the pencil holder Terence had swept off Maggie's desk with his gesture, "but you give too much credit to the politicians. I don't think they can pull it off this time, and I'm encouraging people to go into solar and geothermal, or even into syn-fuels. Anything but petroleum."

Constance had caught the pencil holder on the fly, but upside down. As Maggie knelt to pick up the pencils scattered across the hardwood floor, the two moved their argument toward Terence's office. "Oh, Maggie!" Constance turned back. "You had a phone call while you were out. It's there in the holder."

CHAPTER 3

The call was from Sondra. When Maggie returned the call, Sondra sounded as subdued as she had been the night before, maybe even more so. "How're you doing?" Maggie asked apprehensively, hoping her friend wasn't sinking into a serious depression.

"Oh, I'm all right. It's just that I don't want to leave Yertle just now, and I was wondering if you could stop by the store for me on the way home. It's sort of an emergency."

"Sure," said Maggie, surprised that in her bereavement Sondra felt so hungry. "What can I get for you?"

"Oh, I'm not up to eating anything," said Sondra, as though she had read Maggie's mind, "but I'm out of coffee!"

Maggie shook her head in amazement. She wasn't sure whether to be more relieved (that Sondra was coping well enough to be thinking about coffee) or worried (that she was too obsessed with the dead turtle to walk or drive the few blocks to the store). But she assured her friend that she would be happy to pick up a pound of freshly-ground coffee, having planned a stop at the grocery store on the way home anyway.

Hanging up the phone and returning to her work, Maggie quickly polished off a few more letters and then gave her attention to a research project for Constance involving several mutual funds. She enjoyed the research, finding it more stimulating than many of the more routine tasks, and the afternoon flew by.

As Maggie pulled out of the going-home traffic into the parking lot of the small shopping center near her home, she was listing to herself aloud the items she needed to buy: "Sondra's coffee, milk, bread, chicken breasts, and carrots." That's five things, three of them starting with 'c'—"coffee, carrots, chicken, bread, and milk." Or, in alpha-order, "bread, carrots, chicken, coffee, and milk." Maybe in grocery aisle order is better —"carrots, milk, chicken, coffee, bread."

She had learned from experience that five grocery items were about the maximum she could expect to remember without a written list, and then only with some effort. This time the mnemonics worked for the items, but when she got to the check-out counter, she found she had forgotten the reusable mesh shopping bag that resided in the back seat of the car for just such occasions. "Paper, please," she responded to the bag boy, with a guilty shrug.

The late afternoon sun had warmed the car enough by the time Maggie came out of the grocery store that she rolled down the window immediately, thanking the recycling gods for the hundredth time for non-power windows. Her car, bought used four years ago, was too old to have those push button windows that only worked when the ignition was on. So while she was doing the ecologically correct thing by re-cycling someone else's old car ("pre-owned," the dealer had called it), she got the bonus of being able to open or close a window whenever she wanted to, whether the car was running or not. She didn't mind at all winding the little handle; it seemed a small price to pay.

Heading the car toward Sondra's, Maggie turned her mind also toward her friend. If she's in a better frame of mind, should I invite her down for supper? she wondered. There wouldn't be enough chicken—did Sondra eat chicken, anyway? Maggie wasn't sure. She knew Sondra was very careful about what she ate and what she fed her daughters, avoiding red meat and emphasizing organically-grown vegetables and grains. It had struck Maggie before as odd that such a strictly healthy eater as Sondra should be addicted to caffeine when so many others were avoiding the drug altogether. To each her own, she guessed.

Arriving at Sondra's driveway, Maggie couldn't resist the morbid temptation to look for signs of the previous night's accident—turtle blood, perhaps, or pieces of shell. Blessedly, there were none.

Sondra came to the door so quickly she must have been watching out the window for Maggie's arrival. "I'm so glad you're here," she murmured in Maggie's ear, giving her a warm embrace. "Come into the kitchen and I'll start the coffee."

Backing away to hold Sondra at arm's length, Maggie searched her friend's face for signs of her mood. Her eyes were red-rimmed and her face puffy and pale. "How are you?" Maggie inquired solicitously and then held her breath for the reply.

The reply took longer than Maggie could hold her breath. "Come on in," Sondra repeated, taking the can of coffee and leading the way toward her yellow-and-white kitchen. Maggie looked around her as she walked past the sparsely-furnished family room for signs that might be clues to Sondra's state of mind. The rumpled floor cushions in front of the small tv, the overflowing toy box, and Sondra's cluttered drawing table in the corner by the window looked the same as they always did. The small pink sock in the middle of the floor, next to a blue and white flowered bath towel, merely showed that Sondra had been in no mood to tidy up since the events of the night before. The scraggly spider plant sprawling from a hanging planter over the back door needed water by the look of it, but that too was nothing new at Sondra's house.

As she busied herself at the coffee maker, Sondra acknowledged that she had in fact sat with the dead turtle all night, finally falling into exhausted sleep around sunrise. At 9:00 a.m., she had awakened and had begun trying to reach her children in New Mexico. "I had to let them know right away about Yertle," she explained to Maggie as the two of them sat at Sondra's small white kitchen table.

Maggie nodded sympathetically, picturing the two little girls in a strange city far from home, with the father whose unrelenting conflicts with their mother had forced them to make far too many unhappy choices already in their young lives. "And how did they take the news?" she asked.

The rich smell of brewing coffee mingled with the late afternoon sun streaming down the short hall from the living room windows. "I don't think they really took it in," Sondra said, shaking her head sadly. "They've never experienced a death in the family before."

"So she's decided not to bury the turtle until the first of the summer when the girls get home," Maggie explained to Mike that evening. "She wants them to be able to participate, to be sure they face the death and get to grieve properly."

"So what's she going to do with it between then and now?" Mike asked incredulously. "Keep it in the freezer?"

Maggie smiled sadly from the rocking chair where she was hemming a pair of slacks she'd just shortened for herself. Then she raised her eyebrows and shrugged. The smile turned into a grimace. "What can I say? Sondra thought maybe she could just keep it in a box on the back porch, but I convinced her I'd seen dead turtles on the farm and they rot just like any other dead body. So she wrapped it in a plastic bag, wrote "Yertle the Turtle" on it in big black letters, and took it next door and put it in the neighbor's freezer!"

"In the Clements' freezer? I don't believe it. Dorothy Clement wouldn't let a dead animal inside her house unless it was cut into filets! Or maybe skinned and made into a coat."

"No, no, not the Clements," Maggie hastened to explain. "Nora Patterson, the neighbor on the other side. I don't really know her, but we know a lot of the same people. She goes to some spiritual growth group that Sondra knows about in Kansas City. In fact, she was getting ready to go up there for the weekend.

"She seems pleasant, if a little high strung. Her big old freezer was so full we had to re-pack one side to make room on top. I wonder how she's going to like looking at that dead turtle every time she lifts the lid of the freezer. She evidently doesn't eat meat—at least the freezer was mostly full of vegetables and fruits she'd frozen herself, in plastic cartons. And nuts—lots of nuts in paper packets. Nora has almost quit eating entirely, Sondra told me. Just fruit juice and almonds, some kind of a spiritual discipline."

"Maybe she's a fruitarian," seventeen-year-old Geoff contributed, on his way from the kitchen back to his room with a cold Coke. "You know, eating only fruits."

"What about the almonds? They aren't fruit," his father said.

"Technically, I suppose they're seeds, not fruit. But almond fruit isn't edible, is it?" Maggie said half to herself. "I don't know what Nora is, but she's thin as a rail. Tiny, shorter than I am, and so thin you can almost see through her."

"Needs to eat some meat," Mike pronounced. It was his answer to any dietary situation.

"Alyssa says meat eaters smell funny when you kiss them," Geoff said from the open stairway that ran along the side of the living-room.

"Don't get your dad all stirred up, Geoff," Maggie said firmly. "I'm not in a mood to listen to this discussion. Go on upstairs and quit trying to make trouble."

"Why would anyone want to eat only fruit and nuts?" Mike asked a few minutes later, looking up from his downstairs book to stare at the wall opposite the well-worn sofa where he half-reclined.

"I said I didn't want to get into this conversation," Maggie said, exasperated. "I'm not even a real vegetarian, and I resent being put in the position of defending a lifestyle just because some of my friends and acquaintances choose it."

"No, I'm really trying to understand," Mike said with a air of injured sincerity. "I've been sitting here trying to put myself in that place, and I honestly can't think why anyone would want to do it. I'd get so hungry for some real chewin' meat!"

"Well, briefly, as I understand it, they argue that the digestive tract in humans is most like that of animals that eat only or mostly fruits, so—"

"So, ergo, ips-post facto, and thus, we must eat fodder ourselves." Mike finished Maggie's sentence before she could. Maggie could see he was starting to get his combative juices flowing despite his assurances.

"Ipso facto," she corrected automatically. "There are other reasons. Some people are really determined not to kill anything for food. Fruits are just fruits—they are going to fall off anyway, so if you avoid the seeds, you haven't killed any living thing. Then there's the undeniable fact that fruits taste good. Probably the most widely accepted food by babies, except for mother's milk, of course.

"But let's not talk about this. I don't even know any fruitarians, unless this Nora turns out to be one, and I barely know her. Tell me what you did today. How did your meeting with the Judicial Administrator's Office go?"

"There's good news and bad news," Mike said. "The good news is, the Clerks of the District Court have the coroners' reports on file, going back as far as we could want them, and further. The Judicial Administrator is happy to work with us, and the Clerks would probably be pleased to turn the responsibility for keeping the reports over to someone else."

"Well, duh!" Maggie rolled her eyes. "I could have told you that! It's just one more minor headache."

"The question is," Mike continued unfazed, "who could and would take over the job, and also be able to put the information we want in a data base?"

"Couldn't you get copies from the Clerks, or directly from the Coroners, and create your own data base?" Maggie asked.

"Well, that's where the bad news comes in. In most counties all they have is paper files, indexed by name and by date. There are no electronic files, and as to cause of death, there aren't even *paper* indexes.

"Also, the District Coroners in the cities have detailed notes that are fairly consistent, at least in terms of what they call various things, but these small town doctors who are the county coroners out in God's Country USA seem like they each have their own way of saying it. And even with the coroners in the cities, sometimes you have to read the whole report to find out exactly what happened."

"Well," Maggie said, trying to look for the bright side, "so it may take a little longer, but you can still do the project, can't you?"

"I'm afraid that's what the Director is going to say. It's his pet. But realistically, you're probably talking about a trained medical secretary at least, to read and interpret these things and fit each one into a useful classification system. Something that would work for us. I was hoping we just had to get the reports and have a data entry person pick up the cause of death from the front page—name, date, and county, zip, zip and on the next. Even if we hired extra people it would be years before we'd have a usable file. And then it would only be as useful as the interpretation. I just don't think it's going to be practical."

Maggie frowned, as she was wont to do when concentrating. "I can see that what a doctor would call the cause of death might not be exactly what you law enforcement types would want. But I thought—I mean, where do the figures come from, like national statistics on how many people die of heart attacks, or from drunk driving, or guns. There must be some kind of consistent record-keeping for things like this, or where do all those numbers come from?"

"I asked that myself. But those are pulled by the Department of Vital Statistics from the death certificates—well, at least the heart attacks and that sort of thing. There's a death certificate filed for every death in the state, attended or unattended. The coroner only gets involved when there is an unattended death or for some other reason there might be some question of how or why the subject died. So what we were looking for was a much smaller number of cases, and the information just isn't readily available in the specificity and consistency we would like."

"So what would it take," Maggie asked, "to make the reports in the future useful to you?"

"To make them so we could computerize them? They'd have to use clear, consistent terms that we could organize systematically. Like maybe, "gunshot," and then where in the body and what type of gun, so that a data entry girl could pick up words and enter them without having to be a forensics expert."

Data entry *operator*, Maggie thought, but didn't say aloud. "And how could you get them to do that—the coroners, I mean?"

"It would take a state statute change, and I don't even want to think about trying to get that through," Mike sighed. "It's such a major undertaking even to get changes everyone in law enforcement agrees on. There's always somebody opposed—like the courts, for example, or the lawyers."

"Or the criminals!" Maggie laughed, tossing a small pillow at Mike's head. "Are you getting about ready to think about bed?"

"Yeah, just let me finish this chapter, and I'll be ready," he responded, his attention already back on the biography of Carl Jung he was reading.

A few minutes later Maggie lay beside Mike as he settled in for another hour or so of reading, this time with his upstairs book, a John Le Carré novel. "You know," Maggie said sleepily, "it makes me wonder how good those coroners are across the state. If they don't write consistent reports, does that mean they don't really know what they are doing?"

"Some of them don't," Mike said, without putting down his book.

"Isn't that something to worry about? I mean, should we be alarmed? Shouldn't somebody get excited?"

"It really doesn't matter much. In those rural counties, there's very little violent crime, and what there is, is mostly domestic, pretty obvious. The coroners in the cities like Wichita and the two Kansas City counties do an adequate job, unless they get too busy."

"I'm not sure that's very reassuring," Maggie said. "What about our local coroner here? Is he or she any good?"

"Um. Good night." Mike rolled up on his right shoulder and gently kissed his wife on the lips. He rolled back again and picked up his book.

"In other words, 'shut up and go to sleep,'" Maggie interpreted. It was an old joke. "Good night," she murmured, giving her pillow a push and closing her eyes.

CHAPTER 4

Friday morning dawned with clear skies but a cold edge on the wind. Maggie snagged a nylon on the chair leg at breakfast and the day went downhill from there. At the office, she discovered Terence had forgotten to bring a new can of coffee as promised earlier in the week. There was not quite enough remaining to make one pot, and Maggie's decision to make a full pot anyway earned her grumbles from Constance who complained the brew was too weak.

A client of Nelson's called to complain about not having received a statement of interest on one of his bonds for tax purposes—but he refused to talk to Nelson when Maggie assured him she couldn't assist him in the matter. "I guess he didn't want it fixed, he just wanted to bitch!" Maggie shrugged.

She called Mike mid-morning to cancel lunch since she would have to go buy coffee and stamps.

"Hi, Tiger, I was just about to call you," he said cheerfully, when he heard her voice. "How's your day going?"

You don't want to know," Maggie grumped.

"That bad, huh?" Mike said. "Well, then, maybe this isn't the best time to ask you a favor."

"Oh, go ahead," Maggie said, "everyone else does."

"I was wondering if you could use your contacts with the Clerks of Court to feel them out on computerizing the coroners' reports, with the kind of indexing we'd need."

"I thought the Judicial Administrator had said they wouldn't want to," Maggie said.

"They did," Mike acknowledged. "But the Director thinks

the Clerks might go for it if they got new staff and maybe some new computers out of the deal. And if the Clerks of the local courts are for it, he thinks the J.A. would probably go along. I have to try."

"I can ask around," Maggie said. "But I'm almost certain what the answer will be. These folks are experienced public administrators in their own right. They know the relative value of promises of more help vs. the certainty of more work."

"If you'd see what you can do—maybe get me a meeting with their executive committee?"

"You mean the KBI wants to meet with the officers of the Kansas Association of District Court Clerks and Administrators?" Maggie spoke with mocking emphasis.

"Yeah, I need to," Mike said levelly. "Do you want to help me? Or not?"

"Sure, I can make a couple of phone calls, if it will help you," Maggie said. "At least find out who the current president is and get you a number to call. But I really don't think they are going to be interested in taking on your project."

"Anything you can do," Mike said. "I have to at least make the contact. And since I'm making an end run on the judicial bureaucracy, I can't very well ask the JA's office to put me in touch. See you at lunch, then?"

"Oh!" Maggie said, "the reason I called was I can't make lunch. I have to go run errands."

"So I guess I'll see you this evening, then," Mike said.

By noon, low, dark clouds had moved in from the northwest, and the wind seemed even colder. Maggie clutched her jacket around her and bent her head into the wind as she trudged back from the post office.

In the afternoon, Constance's and Terence's phones started ringing randomly with nobody on the other end, an important letter to an advisory service in New York came back marked INSUFFICIENT POSTAGE ("blankety-blank cheap postal service glue"), and Maggie lost a half-day's work spent typing up final versions of three possible retirement scenarios for Terence, only to have the prospective client call and cancel his appointment.

"All in all, I feel just like the little boy in the Judith Viorst story. I've had a terrible, horrible, no good, very bad day," she whimpered to Mike when they both got home. She nestled her head against his broad chest as he squeezed her close and stroked her head gently.

"There, there," Mike said in a tone of exaggerated sympathy. "It'll be all right. How would you like to go out to eat tonight?"

Maggie lifted her head. "That sounds like an excellent idea!"

"Then we could maybe go to a movie…or we could come home" (Mike backed up a half-step and raised his eyebrows suggestively) "and maybe find something else to do."

Maggie burst out laughing. "We could, huh! Well, we'll see about that, sir!" She cocked her head and looked him out of half-closed eyes. "We'll have to see about that," she repeated. She ran the tip of her tongue slowly along her lips in what she hoped was a ravishingly seductive fashion.

"I suppose Geoff is not eating with us," Maggie continued, dropping the pose as quickly as she had assumed it.

"No, he's got a pizza party at somebody's house. Todd, I think," Mike replied, moving off to pick up the morning paper from the living room floor. "I'll bring this along, shall I, and we can look at the movie possibilities?"

"Sure. We could always go to a movie after dinner, and then still come home and…" Maggie smiled at her husband as she let her voice trail off. It was a source of deep joy and not a little wonder that he still found her desirable and exciting after all these years. "Just give me a minute and I'll be ready to go."

"Better bring an umbrella," Mike called from the carport as Maggie started out the door a few minutes later. "It's starting to drizzle."

By the time they reached the restaurant the drizzle had turned into a hard, cold rain with intermittent bright lightning flashes and loud booms of thunder. "Early in the season for thunderstorms," Mike noted, as they splashed across the parking lot toward McFarlands, the "home cooking" restaurant Mike favored when Geoff was not along. (Geoff despised what he called "old people's restaurants.")

Over roast beef and Swiss steak respectively, Mike and Maggie consulted the movie listings in the *Topeka Capital-Journal*. Nothing sounded worth traipsing around in the weather, so after coffee, they headed home. "Like the rest of the old people," Maggie said.

"You think so?" Mike responded, as he wheeled the car into the carport. A crack of thunder obliterated his next comment, as lightning lit the sky behind the house.

"Whew! That was too close for comfort!" Maggie said, sniffing the air as she got out of the car. "I don't smell anything burning, anyway."

"Never fear, my lady," said Mike, gallantly swinging the house door wide. "I will protect you. Just step into my castle, won't you?"

"I'm forever in your debt, brave sir! Anything I have is yours," Maggie said coyly, deliberately brushing her breast and her hip against Mike as she went through the door.

The rest of the weekend passed quickly. The rain, with occasional bursts of strong wind, thunder, and lightning, continued through Friday night, tapering off to a drizzle Saturday morning and rising again to a steady, roof-drumming downpour Saturday afternoon and all day Sunday.

The houses on the east side of Yew Street had a tendency to flood when the water table rose. The uphill slope behind was steep enough to result in lots of runoff, yet the front lawns were too flat to drain well. Mike's beloved patio was the usual source of concern at the Tenwhistle residence. If rain was falling faster than it could drain away, it would begin coming into the kitchen through the sliding glass doors. Fortunately, there had been less of that since they'd had the new drains put in, but everyone in the family could be seen from time to time peering anxiously through the rain for reassurance that they were not about to be innundated.

Maggie kept busy with household chores until Sunday afternoon, when she declared herself tired of working and took up residence in her favorite easy chair to read a novel Mike had brought home from the library. She'd learned over the years that she was able to face Monday morning much more cheerfully if she worked early in the weekend and saved time for a peaceful Sunday p.m. than if she loafed on Saturday and tried to make up for it Sunday evening.

Even so, Monday morning nearly always came too early, and this one was no exception. But at least the sun was shining for a change! On the way to work, Maggie found herself whistling "get me to the church on time." Not exactly appropriate, she thought, unless you considered the offices of BTH to be a temple of high finance. She chuckled. She'd have to try that out on Terence when he got to the office.

When Terence actually arrived, however, Maggie's little joke was immediately completely forgotten. "Have you heard the news, Maggie?" he demanded urgently as soon as he came in the door. "It's right in your neighborhood, I think."

"What is, Terence? What are you talking about?"

"A lady shot to death. In the Westwood area, on Yew. Isn't that your street?"

"It is! Oh, dear! Do you know who it was, or the address?"

"My impression was it was close to you, 4200's or so. And the name was something like Peterson. Nothing else was disturbed in the house, and they're calling it a possible suicide."

CHAPTER 5

"It was Nora Patterson, Sondra's neighbor I met last week," Maggie told Mike at lunch. "The radio said she was shot with a handgun, and the police have not ruled out the possibility of deliberate suicide. I can't believe it! I just met her last—was it Thursday? Yes, last Thursday evening."

"Was she a good friend of Sondra's," Mike asked.

"Well, they've been next-door neighbors for several years, I guess," Maggie said. She pursed her lips and cocked her head to one side. "They seemed to be on fairly close terms when we were over there. But I've never heard Sondra talk about her. Come to think of it, that's kind of odd, isn't it? If they are friends, and being right next door, you'd think I'd have heard of her or even met her before.

"I wonder if I should call Sondra," Maggie mused, frowning.

"Won't she be at the museum?" Mike reminded.

"Of course she will. And she very likely won't even have heard yet. I'll just wait until I get home. Maybe I'll cook something and take it down. I think Nora has—had—at least one child still here in town, and I suppose there'll be other family coming in."

The local evening tv news covered the story in more detail than had been available in the morning. "The body of the deceased was found by the police at about 8:30 a.m.," said a fresh-faced young reporter who stood in front of Nora's house, his hair blowing into his eyes. "This reporter interviewed a coworker, Arnold Watch, who said he arrived at the Patterson house at around 7:45."

"We always carpool to work, Nora and Joan Grounds and I." The camera switched to a short, balding man in red-framed spectacles, speaking into the reporter's microphone. "Joan and I were right on time. When Nora didn't come out, I went up and knocked on the door. I knocked several times, really loud. Then I tried the door. It was locked, and so were the garage and the back door. We made quite a racket, and then we drove down to the gas station on the corner and tried phoning her.

"It wasn't like Nora to be gone without letting us know." The man was becoming more agitated as he spoke, and his voice rose in pitch. "When she didn't answer the phone, we called 911 and went back to wait for the police." He turned his head away from the camera.

"Thank you, Mr. Watch," the reporter said quickly. Pictures of police cars followed, with an ambulance standing in the drive. Then a sheet-covered stretcher could be seen being loaded into the ambulance, while the reporter's voice went on giving details. The body had been found in the dining room, with a small caliber handgun nearby. Police were still investigating. An autopsy was to be performed to determine the time and cause of death.

"Don," the anchorwoman's voice interrupted, "Don, can you tell us whether there was any sign of forced entry?"

"None, Jane," the reporter replied, his face reappearing on the screen, now against the background of a large evergreen tree, which stood between the house and the street. From the long shadows, it was clear this shot was live, in contrast with the previous shots from earlier in the day. "Police say also there is no sign of robbery or struggle. No one is either confirming or denying that the death may have been a suicide; however, if a suicide note was found, officials are not admitting it."

"Thank you, Don," said the anchorwoman. "We'll be keeping our viewers up to date on this situation. Tune in for the News at Ten when we hope to bring you more."

"Whoa, man! Right here on our own street!" Geoff exclaimed. "Do we know this person?" he asked his parents.

"Mom does, slightly," Mike replied with a warning glance.

"It's okay," Maggie said. "I'm not emotionally involved. I'm interested is all. She didn't seem depressed or anything when I met her. And she was all excited about this weekend workshop she was going to in Kansas City. Something pretty heavy must have happened up there if she came home and killed herself.

"I'm a little concerned about Sondra. She may have gone to that workshop too, for all I know. Who knows how she's taking this, on top of everything else. I think I'll go call her." Maggie stood up and started toward the kitchen.

"Are we about ready to eat?" Geoff asked. "I have a lot of homework tonight."

"You could set the table and get people something to drink," Maggie said, lifting the phone from the wall. "And grate some cheese for the spaghetti. Everything else is ready, and I won't be very long." She smiled to herself as she dialed Sondra's number. Geoff had walked right into that one.

After dinner, Geoff excused himself quickly and headed up to his room, whence could soon be heard the strains of his latest Paul Simon album. Mike announced his intentions to wash the dishes.

Maggie located the cookbook that came with the microwave and turned to the vegetable section. "I heard from somebody that it's pretty easy to make au gratin potatoes in the microwave," she told Mike. "And I need to take something down to Nora's house. Sondra says the daughters and the ex-husband are all there at the house, and out-of-town relatives are coming tomorrow. So I'd like to take something down and go over with Sondra, just to be supportive."

"Couldn't be you're a little bit curious, too, could it?" Mike teased.

"An old criminal court clerk? Nah! Don't be silly!" Maggie

and Mike had first met when she was working in the Ford County criminal court in Dodge City and he was a young deputy sheriff testifying in an armed robbery trial. That was long before they moved east to Lindsborg, before Mike joined the Bureau, before even Mike had finished college.

"I'm going purely to perform my social duty as a neighbor of the departed," Maggie said, slicing potatoes into a casserole dish. "And if I accidentally pick up any good gossip, I'll just keep quiet about it because I'm sure you wouldn't want to know anything about it. Would you now?"

Half an hour later, Maggie was standing outside Sondra's front door, balancing a hot casserole on two thick potholders. She kicked the storm door gently, hoping the resulting noise sounded enough like a knock to get Sondra's attention.

A musical tinkle came from the small brass bell that hung by a red cord from the door handle. Sondra had explained once that the bell had been intended to allow the family cat to announce when he wanted in. But the cat almost never used it, and the bell continued to hang there looking out of place, an exotic bit of flotsam on the front of this otherwise bland American-modern facade with its imitation wrought iron decoration.

When Sondra opened to the door, she was wiping her hands on a dishtowel. "Come in," she said. "Here, let me take that." She reached for the dish in Maggie's hands.

"Better let me," Maggie cautioned. "It's very hot." Sondra led the way through the family room to the kitchen. Taking a wood-and-brass trivet from a drawer, Sondra placed it on the light yellow countertop. Maggie set down her burden with a sigh of relief.

The two embraced. "What an awful thing!" Maggie began.

"I can't believe it, I really can't," said Sondra in a rush of words. "I mean, I can't believe she would have shot herself. The woman is—was—a pacifist, for goodness sake! She was totally non-violent. I know for a fact that not only would she not kill ants or flies in her house, but she quit raising lettuce last year because she said she couldn't stand to hear them screaming when she cut the heads."

"Was anything troubling her, do you know?" ventured Maggie.

"No, but I really didn't see much of her. We talked over the back yard fence in summer mostly."

"I thought maybe you'd gone to KC with her this weekend," said Maggie, leaning against a cabinet.

"Oh, no. She did invite me, but I've sort of stayed away from gurus in general and this one in particular. She was riding with Leslie Stone." Sondra snapped the top off a can of frozen orange juice concentrate and plopped its contents into a gallon jar nearly full of pinkish liquid. "Just let me stir this up and I'll be ready to go."

"I've been concerned about you," Maggie said, watching Sondra's long-handled spoon chase a bright glob of orange around and around the bottom of the jar, which sat in one half of the double stainless steel sink. "I mean, your loss last week and then this..."

"Well, to tell you the truth...now, this is going to sound awful, but...well, I mean." Sondra stopped stirring and turned toward Maggie. "Oh, I'm so glad you understand, Maggie. So many people wouldn't. To them, any animal is just an animal." She turned back to the jar. "Yertle was so special. He used to crawl down on my table when I'd be painting and sit in the sun, and I swear he was watching every brush stroke."

She was stirring very slowly now. "Or I'd put him in the sandbox with Bo and Claire and he'd play with them. He put out such a loving spirit. He wasn't just a turtle. It's awfully hard to..." Sondra removed the spoon from the jar, wiped the corner of each eye with her sweatshirt sleeve, and took a deep breath. Then, putting a lid on the jar, she straightened and announced briskly, "I'm ready to go."

Together they walked up the small terrace that separated

the Patterson house from its neighbor on the south. A maroon Buick sedan sat in the driveway, overshadowed by one of two huge red cedar trees. A nondescript light green subcompact sat on the street in front of the two-story brick house. "You know, Maggie," Sondra said as they walked up the short curving sidewalk, "I'll have to get Yertle out of Nora's freezer. I'd better do that tonight, don't you think?"

Sondra hugged the gallon jar of punch with one arm and pushed the doorbell button with the other hand. She stepped back, and the two stood expectantly, looking at the amber glass panels on either side of the door. After a few moments, the door was opened by a slender, dark-haired young woman in fashionably-flared blue jeans and a tailored white blouse. She peered out at them in the fading twilight.

"Hello, Karin. I don't know if you remember me. I'm Sondra Sampson. I live next door. And this is Maggie Tenwhistle, another neighbor. We're so very sorry about your mother." Sondra held out the jar of fruit punch in both hands.

"We brought some things over," Maggie added when the young woman continued to stand silently in the doorway looking at them as though she didn't comprehend.

"Oh, yes," she finally responded, as if awakening from a stupor. "Well, uh, thank you. Won't you come in?" She stepped back and gestured politely.

"If you're sure we're not intruding?" Maggie hesitated on the threshold.

"Oh, no, not at all. Orin's here, my dad, that is, and Kara...." Her voice trailed off.

Sondra stepped briskly down the hall to the kitchen, the other two trailing behind. "Karin lives in—Omaha, is it?" she said brightly, turning her head to include both Karin and Maggie.

"Yes, Omaha," was the dull reply.

"She's a nurse. Right?"

"An OB nurse, yes," Karin answered with a bit more life in her voice. "I love it."

"Can we just put these things in the fridge?" Sondra asked. "Or would you want to use them now? This is some fruit punch, and Maggie's brought…."

" Potatoes," said Maggie on cue. "Au gratin potatoes. They can be frozen and heated up any time." She held out the casserole.

"Oh, hello, Sondi!" The cheerful voice in the doorway belonged to another slender, dark-haired young woman in jeans.

"Kara, dear." Sondra set down the jar of punch to swoop forward and embrace the girl tenderly. "I'm so very sorry."

"Thanks. It's quite a shock, I can tell you." The enthusiasm in this girl's voice and face contrasted oddly with her sister's pallor and subdued manner, especially since they looked so much alike otherwise. She turned to Maggie with a gracious smile. "Here, let me take that. Thank you so much. I'll just set it on the stove. Maybe someone will want some after a while."

She set the casserole down and returned the potholders to Maggie. Then she looked back at Maggie. "Don't I know you?"

"I don't know," Maggie said, frowning. "I'm Maggie Tenwhistle. I live down the street."

"You're Alyssa Tenwhistle's mother, aren't you?"

"Kara…Patterson? Are you that Kara Patterson? You and Alyssa were in *A Midsummer Night's Dream* together at West. What a surprise!" Maggie smiled broadly. "I didn't—I mean, I hadn't made the connection." Then she continued, more subdued as she recalled the occasion of the visit, "I'm sorry we're not meeting at a happier time."

"Yes," said Kara, with a sudden tone of deep sadness. "As I said, it's a great shock."

For a moment they all stood contemplating their feet. Then Karin interrupted the silence to say, "Won't you come in to the living room and meet our father?"

Orin Patterson was one of the handsomest men she had ever met, Maggie decided immediately as he stood to greet the guests. (Irreverently, she imagined describing him to the

Tuesday night group as "tall with dark wavy hair and a classic profile, a line-backer's broad muscular chest, and a tight end.") Sitting on the gray-blue tailored sofa near him was a quietly attractive woman Maggie guessed to be in her late 40's or early 50's. Karin introduced them as "my father and his wife, Lorraine," her voice dropping noticeably on the last part of the phrase.

    Introductions completed, Orin gestured for everyone to sit down. There were further expressions of shock and sympathy followed by a few minutes' subdued conversation. Maggie and Kara did most of the talking. Kara, Maggie learned, was attending Topeka's Washburn University, majoring in dramatics and living in her own apartment. "I'll be sure to tell Alyssa I saw you," Maggie promised.

    Karin sat sheltered in a wing-back chair, staring into the empty fireplace at the far end of the room. Orin shifted uncomfortably on a sofa too low for his long legs and spoke only occasionally in a rich baritone. Lorraine sat perfectly still beside her husband and spoke not at all.

    About the time Maggie was getting ready to suggest they had to leave, Sondra cleared her throat meaningfully. "Oh, say, Kara," she said, "I had something in your mother's freezer. I'm sorry to trouble you, but could I get it out now?"

    Orin Patterson jumped to his feet as though eager to have something to do. "Let me help you," he said quickly, and led the way to the kitchen.

    "Well, I guess we really should be going." Maggie stood up. "If there is anything I can do to help," she looked from Kara to Karin and back, "don't hesitate to call on me."

    "Thank you," said Karin, standing also. She shook Maggie's hand.

    "Well, goodbye, then," said Maggie, wondering if she should shake hands all around. "I'm glad to have met you, Mrs. Patterson." She nodded in Lorraine's direction.

    "Goodbye, Mrs. Tenwhistle," said Kara. "And thanks for

coming." Abruptly, she threw her arms around Maggie and squeezed her tightly.

Following a sudden impulse, Maggie spoke softly. "You're welcome to come down to the house any time," she said in a voice pitched for Kara's ears only, "if you just need to get away for a while, or someone to talk to."

Kara gave her an unreadable look, which Maggie guessed was covering either gratitude or suspicion, and moved toward the front hall and the outside door.

Maggie followed. The two of them were joined immediately by Sondra and Orin Patterson, coming from the kitchen, Sondra holding a dark, frosty object wrapped in clear plastic.

Outside the door, Maggie and Sondra walked in silence down the terrace to Sondra's house, each absorbed in her own thoughts.

"Do you want to come in for a little while?" Sondra asked as they reached her front door.

"No, I think I'd better go home," Maggie replied. "I'm just wondering about Nora. Do you think she was depressed? How long have she and Orin been divorced?"

"Oh, I don't actually know. Since before we moved into this house, so more than six years anyway. I never really knew Orin."

"Too bad," murmured Maggie. "Too bad."

CHAPTER 6

"I can see where a woman could be suicidal, even after five or six years, if she'd had a man like that and let him get away," she told Mike later. "He has a profile a lot like Cary Grant's, and just a touch of gray at the temples. He's a partner in one of the old, stuffy law firms. It's too bad he doesn't have a trial practice. He'd be hell on wheels with the women on a jury."

"If I'd known you were going to fall in love with the widower—the ex-widower? whatever—if I known you were going to be leering at some man, I'd have come along to protect my interest," Mike complained. "I suppose you didn't learn anything about the deadee, either."

"Before you get all excited, you should know that his wife, his present wife, was there, too. So we were well-chaperoned." Maggie looked fondly at her husband. His straight black hair and strong broad nose reflected his Native American ancestry, but he was taller and more slender than his father, who had grown up on the Prairie Band Pottawatomi reservation north of Topeka. His mother, who was Cherokee, always said there was a Swede or a German back there somewhere on his father's side, and there must have been some truth in it, for their daughter Alyssa had blue eyes like Maggie's own.

"And I did too learn some interesting things." She broke out of her reverie. "But of course you don't want to hear them."

"Ah, but you want to tell them!" Mike chuckled. "So I get to hear them anyway."

"Actually, there wasn't much. Sondra hadn't gone to the Kansas City thing. Nora rode with a guy from Auburn. We talked a bit about what could have happened at the workshop. I took it the family hadn't been too gung ho about her attending these things.

"The leader is some guru from Chicago, a supposedly enlightened being who goes around spreading good cheer and blessings to the faithful. Kara, the younger daughter, had been to one session, and said she didn't like the fellow at all. Thought he was a total flake."

"What would you expect?" Mike interjected. "Can any good come out of Chicago?"

"According to the family, it was her work with Ram Boss or whatever his name is that got Nora convinced that she'd advance faster spiritually if she ate only fruit and nuts. But there's another thing. Sondra says that Nora was completely against violence of any kind. She's just sure she wouldn't have had or even handled a gun. This was a woman who didn't even like killing cockroaches.

"So she—Sondra—doesn't think Nora could possibly have killed herself. She didn't say this in front of the family, of course. They all seemed satisfied with the idea of suicide. Well, you know what I mean. Not 'satisfied,' but not questioning it. Actually, they were all pretty much in shock, I think."

"Do you want to watch the 10:00 news?" Mike asked.

"Sure, we might as well," said Maggie. "Since we're not avoiding gossip, we might as well pick up anything new that's available."

The late news had little to add on the death that hadn't already been made public. Police confirmed no suicide note had been found. The police department had no information on when the autopsy results would be available, and the coroner's office had no comment.

In a separate story, the coroner's office was one of several county departments under fire from the county comptroller for spending more than a quarter of their budget in the first quarter of the year. The head of the roads department explained on camera that the late winter storms had resulted in higher than average expenditures for salt and sand. The register of deeds blamed bookkeeping problems and high turnover during December and January for her difficulties, and said she expected to be back on track by June. The coroner had no comment.

"Nothing about the cause of death yet." Maggie was disappointed. "Say, honey," she said, suddenly remembering. "Speaking of coroners, I got you the name and phone number of the KADCCA president, if you want to call him on your project. He's the Clerk in the Jackson County District Court." Maggie paused, and then plunged ahead shamelessly. "I don't suppose you'd like to return the favor and call one of your buddies at TPD, to see whether they still think it's suicide? Just to satisfy my curiosity?"

"I might see what I can find out in the morning, if you remind me," Mike said laconically. "It's none of the Bureau's business, but unofficially I can probably find out where they are with it. They might even like to know what Sondra said about the lady being a pacifist."

"Now don't you go getting Sondra involved," said Maggie, suddenly alarmed.

"I'm sure they'll be interviewing her anyway, as a matter of course," Mike soothed. "It won't hurt for them to be primed a little as to what to ask. They would take it as a favor from me."

Maggie thought, but didn't say, that it would be a favor to Sondra if she did a little priming of her own. She'd give her friend a warning call in the morning.

When Maggie called her the next morning, Sondra seemed almost unconcerned about the news that she should expect a visit from the police.

"Thanks for letting me know, Maggie," she said. "I wouldn't have thought about it, but I suppose it's natural under the circumstances for them to talk a little more to the neighbors.

"I'm glad you called, anyway. I'm in a terrible rush right

now—almost late to work—but I need your help with Yertle. I find I can't bear having him in the house with me. It's bad enough knowing I ran over him—that it's my fault he's dead. I know my karma and his are all entangled, and I should be doing prayers for his spirit's passage. But I can't stand seeing him lying there every time I open the door of the refrigerator.

"I know it's an awful lot to ask, but could you possibly keep him for me, just until the girls get home? If my freezing section were a little bigger maybe it wouldn't be so bad, but—well, I really can't keep reaching over him every time I need granola or whole wheat flour."

Maggie did the mental equivalent of a double-take. The nerve of some people! "Actually," she stalled, "my freezing section isn't that much bigger than yours." She wrinkled her nose in distaste.

"I suppose," she continued reluctantly, glad Sondra couldn't see her expression over the phone, "if—could you wrap it again, I mean, over the plastic, with something opaque? Maybe aluminum foil, or some kind of freezer paper? I think…sure, that would be okay, I guess. If you'd just wrap it in something. Just for a few weeks, right? You'd be burying it just as soon as the girls get home?"

"Yes, sure, of course!" Sondra agreed quickly. "I always know I can count on you, Maggie, and I do appreciate it so much! Thank you for being such a dear! Now I have to run. Bye-bye."

Maggie hung up the phone and sighed. She opened the top door of her refrigerator to look at the freezer compartment. The turtle couldn't use up that much room, she guessed. But she still felt taken advantage of, and annoyed with herself for letting it happen.

On the way to work, Maggie made a point of listening to the news in case there was anything more on Nora Patterson's death. There wasn't. Just a repeat of what had been reported the night before. When Terence Hannigan arrived at the office, he was predictably eager to compare notes with Maggie. "Did you know the woman?" he asked.

"Just slightly," Maggie said. "She was a neighbor of a friend of mine. And my daughter was in school with her daughter, a year behind, although I didn't know it. I mean, I hadn't made the connection between the mother and the daughter until last night."

"Then you've talked to the family," Terence said, a gleam in his eye. "How are they handling it?"

"Very well, so far as I could tell," Maggie said reluctantly. (It didn't seem quite right, gossiping about someone else's misfortune this way.) "I mean, as well as could be expected. Her children are grown, her ex-husband has remarried. It's hard to tell—I don't know these people."

She found herself reviewing the previous evening's encounter. "Everybody was pretty quiet, except for maybe the younger daughter. If anything, she seemed a little hyper now that I think about it."

"If you need to take off to go to the funeral, just let us know," Constance interrupted solicitously on the way back from her second trip to the coffee pot.

"I don't think so," Maggie said. "Or else, maybe, if my friend needs someone to go with her. I should probably check. Thanks."

"Do you know when the services are?" Terence asked.

"Probably tomorrow, or maybe Thursday," said Maggie uncertainly. "I suppose it depends on when the autopsy is done and the body released. Maybe Friday. I expect these people would want to have a simple burial, as soon as possible."

"Just let us know," Constance repeated from her doorway. "If you need to be with your friend, you need to be there."

In the mid-afternoon, turning away from the client file on the computer screen to rest her eyes, Maggie noticed the reception area had grown unusually dark. She flipped on the second bank of lights, now rarely used since she had pointed out to her employers that she had plenty of light over her desk and anyone sitting in the waiting area could read by the light of the high west-facing windows. She stepped to the windows now and looked out at blue-black clouds rising from the horizon high into the sky. No doubt, she speculated glumly, the rain would hold off until about 5:00, and then the deluge.

In fact, the rain began around 4:00 and was still coming down fast and furiously as Maggie stood in the red-tiled entryway at the back of the Fountain Building at 5:10. She looked through the ornately engraved glass of the restored 1880's door at the water running down the middle of the alley. Too bad the rumor of a covered walkway had never materialized. Oh, well, she thought, as she splashed across to the parking garage, thank goodness for covered parking, at least.

As Maggie approached Sondra's house on her way home, she slowed and then pulled into the driveway. Might as well get this turtle business out of the way. She got out of the car and dashed for Sondra's front door. Under the shelter of the roof overhang, she reached for and rang the cat bell. She stood watching the water cascade down the slope from the Patterson house, across Sondra's front lawn and into the gutter, now running level with the curb.

The rain had slowed to a heavy sprinkle, but it was still blowing in under the roof as the wind gusted strongly from the west. After a wait of probably not long enough, Maggie rang the bell again, harder.

"Come in, come in! You look a little wet!" Sondra exclaimed, holding the door open wide.

"I can't stay. I'm on my way home, and I just thought I'd stop and pick up, uh, Yertle, you know, if you really still want me to, uh, store him for you." Maggie made no attempt to keep her lack of enthusiasm from showing in her voice.

"Yes, great! Thanks!" Sondra said, either oblivious to or determined to ignore Maggie's discomfort. "Come on in. I've been fighting the water ever since I got home at 4:30." Maggie noticed for the first time that Sondra was barefoot and wearing only a tank top and a sarong tied at the waist as a short skirt.

Both garments were decidedly damp.

"You noticed the water running in the front? Well, it runs even worse in the back, and when the ground gets saturated like this, it comes up onto the patio. I've been trying to build a sort of dike to direct it somewhere else and keep it out of the house."

She moved toward the kitchen. "Now that the rain's letting up, I'm hoping it will be okay. Just have a chair. I'll get Yertle in just a minute. Would you like some coffee?" Sondra nodded toward the half-filled pot on the counter. "It's fresh."

"No, thanks," Maggie said, standing by the table. I really have to go."

Sondra, who had already started to pour coffee into a grey-brown mug with a bright yellow sunflower on the side, set the half-filled mug down quickly and moved to the refrigerator. "Right! Of course."

"If you are ready for me to take him, that is," Maggie said, uncertain whether she was precipitating another crisis or just dealing with Sondra's usual distractibility.

"Oh, yes, please!" Sondra said quickly, opening the door to the freezing section at the top of the refrigerator. She turned around, holding the still plastic-wrapped turtle in her palms like an Egyptian attendant bearing the royal offering into the burial chamber.

"I'd really like it double-wrapped, if you don't mind, before I put it in my freezer," Maggie said weakly. Then, seeing the anxiety on Sondra's face, she continued rather more forcefully, "I could do it myself, if you'd rather."

"Whatever," said Sondra, sounding far away. "It isn't right to shuffle him around like this, I know. I've sensed his spirit still near the body, and I should be strong enough to stay with him and help him go. But I just can't do it.

"When we went over to Nora's, I felt him there, and I thought it would be good to have him home. But when Orin leaned over and lifted him out of the bottom of that big freezer, when he picked him up, I felt this—like a real disturbance in his spirit. Yertle's, I mean. And it hasn't settled down the whole time he's been back here with me.

"So please take him, and keep him safe for me." She glided toward Maggie, still holding the package on her outstretched hands.

Wondering what she might be letting herself in for, Maggie took the turtle from Sondra and turned to leave. Then she turned back. "I meant to ask—do you know when the funeral is, and do you want me to go with you? I mean, do you need me to go along?"

"I hadn't really thought that far," Sondra mused. "If they even have a funeral. They may not, unless Nora's family, her parents or whoever, insist. When we used to talk about such things..." Sondra seemed to be looking at something miles away, over Maggie's right shoulder. "I mean, both Nora and Orin would probably prefer no ceremony, just a simple burial, or more likely cremation, and the ashes sprinkled outdoors somewhere. Ceremonies are for the living, not the dead. To say goodbye...."

Her voice trailed off. Maggie realized Sondra was staring at the frozen object she held, now beginning to drip slightly as frozen condensation started to melt.

"Well, I'd better get home." Maggie indicated the package containing the frozen turtle. "I'll keep this for you till the girls get home."

"Yes. Thank you," said Sondra. "I hope you are okay with this. You'd say if you were uncomfortable? It's a great help to me." She suddenly looked so forlorn Maggie felt ashamed of her earlier uncharitable thoughts.

"So, okay. Sure!" Maggie cleared her throat. "I'd better let you get back to your water. Be sure and call us if you need a hand."

"Right, thanks again. I guess I'd better. Can you let yourself out?"

Maggie let herself out. The rain had nearly stopped, although the still-dark sky suggested the respite might not last long. Maggie laid her burden on the front seat of the car on a sheet of newspaper plucked from a sackful in the back. She'd forgotten to stop at the recycler to leave off the two weeks' collection of newspapers. All the extra gas used hauling them around probably offset any environmental good it did to recycle! She sighed as she pulled out of Sondra's drive and headed for home.

Once there, Maggie dug a couple of old pieces of aluminum foil out of a kitchen drawer and smoothed them out before molding them around the plastic-encased reptile. She tore off a long strip of masking tape and stuck it on the package. "T-U-R-T-L-E," she printed in red marker. "Do Not Thaw! Do NOT Open!"

"Mom, what are we doing for dinner," Geoff called from the stairway. "I'd like to go to Valentino's. Dad says he doesn't care."

"I said I'd be glad to do whatever your mother wanted," Mike corrected from the living room. "Would you like to go out, Maggie, or did you have something planned?"

"I would love to go out!" Maggie said fervently. She closed the door to the freezer compartment where she had carefully tucked the turtle under three loaves of homemade bread on the left-hand side. "But I don't know that I'm up for pizza."

"How about Chinese?" Mike suggested.

"No, not Chinese," Maggie responded quickly, as an old memory of a Chinatown luncheonette featuring duck feet, fish lips, and other assorted animal parts rose unbidden to her mind. "Not tonight. How about Bennigan's?"

"Bennigan's is fine with me," said Mike.

"Is that okay, Geoff?" Maggie called.

"Sure, fine." Geoff sounded disappointed, but Maggie didn't feel like negotiating.

Then, suddenly, Maggie clipped her forehead with her palm in the classic "Dummkopf" gestures. "Hey, guys, forget everything I just said!" she said "You two can do whatever you want for dinner. I have my group tonight, and I'll have to hustle around to fix something to take."

CHAPTER 7

"I haven't seen Sondi for months," Anna Prince said, reaching for another muffin. "How is she taking Nora's death?"

"She didn't seem much affected, I thought," Maggie said. "I got the impression she didn't know Nora all that well. I was asking her opinion about the suicide theory and she talked like she really didn't see much of her. And I don't remember ever hearing her mention Nora before, even though they were next-door neighbors."

Maggie looked around the small oak dining room table at the familiar faces. It was Tuesday night, and the four of them were sharing their regular bi-weekly potluck supper in Laurie's comfortable first-floor apartment. "The Gang of Four," as Mike called them, had been meeting like this for more than five years. Besides Maggie, there were Anna, with the china-doll complexion and strawberry-blond curls, her delicate figure camouflaged tonight in a pair of baggy overalls; Suzanne Coffey, tall and rangy-thin, with short, straight blond hair and piercing blue eyes; and black-haired Laurie Jetts, in a deep wine shirt with ruffled collar and cuffs that made her look more like a 17th century pirate than the radiology tech she was.

"Sondra Sampson has no reason to love Nora Patterson," Laurie said abruptly. "Maybe she knows more than she's saying."

"I always felt she was the 'injured party,' to use that phrase in its rather quaint sense," said Suzanne. "Even though to hear Nora and Sam talk it was just hunky-dory among all three of them."

"You mean Nora Patterson is the woman Sam Sampson

was seeing before he and Sondra separated?" Maggie was stunned.

"You didn't know? It was soon after Sondi and Sam moved to the West Hills area," Laurie said. "Orin Patterson had been gone about a year, I suppose."

"I'm surprised you didn't know," Suz said, tilting her chin and squinting at Maggie through wire-rimmed glasses. "Everyone did."

"I didn't know Sondra in those days. What, four or five years ago? We were moving in different circles then. So anyway, tell me the rest of the story."

"Well," Suz began, passing a plate of avocado slices and strawberries to Maggie, "Orin and Nora had an 'open marriage'—and they were very open about that fact! At least, Nora was. She slept with half the guys in the co-op, one time or another, I'd guess, and it didn't matter to her whether they were married themselves or not."

"It was a part of the liberation process, as she explained it," Anna continued thoughtfully. "If you couldn't feel good about yourself sexually, and free to love whoever you loved, then how could you go on to clear out all the rest of the old baggage? How could you heal?" She stared at her bran muffin as though she expected it to answer.

Laurie picked up the story. "When Sondi and Sam moved into the house next door, Nora was only too eager to be a good neighbor. She introduced them around, got them started in the co-op. Her girls—well, Kara at least, Karin was already in college, I think—Kara babysat the babies when they came. And after a while folks started noticing Nora and Sam were together more than Nora and Sondi."

"Or Sondi and Sam," Suz contributed.

"Sam never actually moved in with Nora," Laurie continued, "but he apparently spent a whole lot of time over there for a while. Nora was doing a lot of stuff with crystals at the time, and she was teaching a class at her house on healing with crystals that Sam purported to find utterly fascinating."

Laurie's husky voice dripped sarcasm.

"I remember a conversation in which Sondi was trying to explain how it was all so honest, and what good friends they all were, when everyone else in the room could see that she was hurting so much she could hardly see straight," Suz said softly. "It sounds so good in theory and works out so painfully in practice!"

"So?" Maggie prompted.

"So, after a while, Sam and Nora cooled off, but by then the damage had been done. Sondi and Sam stayed together for another year or so, and then he left. And you know the rest," Laurie concluded.

"That's a sad story," Maggie said. "And a confusing one, too, I guess. I've been a one-man woman for so long, I can't imagine what it would be like to be otherwise. But it does seem a good idea—being able to have physical expressions of love at all levels of intimacy, from a hand shake to—whatever. Maybe I'm just totally naive."

"That could be, too," Laurie laughed. Then she turned serious again. "But it's the screwed-up patriarchal system that's to blame. We've all been taught that marriage involves ownership, and even today, we still think that's what it means."

"Maybe so," Suz interjected, "but this is too heavy a subject for dessert. I brought some ice cream. Anybody want some to eat with the rest of those strawberries?"

"So here I am with this blessed turtle in my freezer!" Maggie said ten minutes later, licking the last of the ice cream from her spoon. "I honestly believe Sondra is more upset about the turtle than she is about Nora. She was up all night that first night, reading the Book of the Dead over it. I guess I could understand a little more if it were a dog or a cat. But so help me, a turtle!"

"More than that," Maggie continued, frowning, "there's something about the situation that makes me uncomfortable."

"Maybe you're picking up the disturbed turtle vibes Sondi

said she was receiving," suggested Anna.

Maggie looked at Anna, trying to determine whether the remark was meant seriously. Anna's pretty, round face wore a look of solemn concern, much like what Maggie imagined her adopting when listening to a client in her practice as a clinical psychologist. But as Maggie continued to stare at her, a mischievous twinkle betrayed the corners of Anna's eyes and mouth.

"Turtle vibes? I *really* don't think so," said Maggie, with a falling inflection. "Besides, it doesn't feel like that. It's more like when you've forgotten something you were supposed to do, or check on, or something."

Laurie stood up and began stacking plates. "That'll give us something to work on tonight, then," she said. "I'll just stick these in the dishwasher real quick. The rest of you go on and get started."

In the adjoining living room, Maggie claimed one corner of the pink-and-white flowered sofa and stretched her feet out to rest her heels on the edge of the oiled oak coffee table. Suz curled her long body around a dark green oversize pillow on the other side of the table, and Anna pulled a wicker basket chair up to one end.

"What are your associations with turtles, Maggie? Maybe that will jar something loose," Anna suggested, fluffing her hair with slender fingers.

Maggie closed her eyes and leaned back against the sofa cushions. In a well-practiced relaxation sequence, she checked her body for lingering tension and let her mind drift to a pleasant, peaceful blankness. After a few moments, eyes still closed, she smiled slowly.

"The first thing that comes to mind is a big snapping turtle we found down by the pond when I was a kid. He was huge, sixteen or eighteen inches across the length of the shell, at least. The pond was running over the spillway after a heavy rain, and my mother took us kids out in our boots to look at him. Now that

I think of it, he may have come up from the river. I don't know how something that big could have grown in our little pond.

"We prodded him with a long stick and he bit the end of the stick right off. Mother assured us he would do the same thing to a finger. I think it was so we'd see why they were called 'snappers.' We were duly impressed."

"What else about turtles?"

"Well, there was one the size of a silver dollar that my brother had when he was about eight. It was green and he kept it in an old fish bowl and fed it lettuce. I don't think it lived very long. I remember something about a bad smell."

"And?" Anna prompted.

"To me, turtles belong outdoors in the mud, and if you try to keep them inside, they die and begin to smell," Maggie said.

"That could be it. Does it feel like it?" Suz inquired.

"No." Maggie opened her eyes. "No, I think that has a lot to do with my not wanting Yertle in my freezer, but I already knew that! I feel like there's still something I'm forgetting."

"Shall we do a card layout on it?" asked Laurie, who had just come from the kitchen.

"Sure," Maggie agreed. She sat up and reached in her bag to pull out a small dark deeply-carved wooden box. Removing the lid, she unfolded a blue silk scarf and lifted out a stack of oblong cards a little larger than regular playing cards. She shuffled the cards several times, and then paused.

"What's the question?" asked Suz.

"The question is, what do I need to know about this unease regarding the turtle situation? Okay?" She looked at Laurie, who was now ensconced in the other corner of the couch, and then at Suz and Anna. Anna nodded.

"Then I'll shuffle that question in." Maggie shuffled the cards thoroughly and cut them into three stacks. She held her hand briefly palm down over each stack in turn, and then selected the center one.

She replaced the other cards in the wooden box and began to deal from the top of the chosen stack. "Here am I," she recited, as she laid out the first card, face up on the coffee table. "This helps me, this crosses me." She laid down two more, each partially overlapping the first card.

"Coming from, going toward," she continued, as she laid the next two cards to the left and right, respectively, of the first trio.

"Underlying." She laid a sixth card below the first grouping. "And the best possible outcome." The seventh card she placed directly above the center of the grouping. "Inner environment, outer environment, hopes and fears, most probable outcome," she chanted quickly, laying four more cards in a line along the right of those already placed. Maggie and the other women surveyed the layout of cards. "This doesn't look too promising," Maggie said.

"Looks like it's going to get worse before it gets better, anyway," commented Suz, pointing to the Nine of Swords. The card pictured a colorful swirl of nightmarish monsters arising from the head of a prone figure surrounded by sword blades. "'Going toward' confusion, nightmare, apparent danger."

"Emphasis on 'apparent,'" said Anna. "Could be just an illusion."

"This is some heavy-duty stuff, Maggie," said Laurie. "Five Major Arcana cards out of eleven."

"With the Devil archetype underlying it all," Maggie observed, looking at the card which pictured several figures chained together and others in various postures of subservience or distress. "That seems to speak to me of oppressive or conflicted relationships. People feeling chained to particular roles and positions and unable to get out."

"Not without either violence or unendurable sacrifice," chimed in Laurie, her finger underlining first two characters fighting one another in one corner of the card and then a tableau which showed a kneeling mother handing her child over to an armed soldier.

"So who does this refer to?" Anna asked after a long

silence.

"All of us," Laurie pronounced. "The patriarchy chains and imprisons us all, and only a cultural change of massive proportions can alter that." Her black pageboy bounced decisively.

"But what does that have to do with my turtle question?" Maggie wailed.

"Laurie sees everything in terms of patriarchy these days," Suz teased.

"Maybe it's Sondi, trapped as a single mother with no one to share the trauma of everyday family crises," Anna said thoughtfully.

"Or me, hooked into helping with this absurd project because I love Sondra even though I can't understand her," Maggie said.

"This is supposed to be you in your present situation, or what it's basically all about," said Suz. "The Five of Discs." She held up the card with a brightly-colored drawing of a woman kneading a mound of something, bread or perhaps clay.

"I often get my best creative insights while kneading bread," Anna said after a moment. "I'm thinking maybe you should just let the situation ferment for a while, let your subconscious knead it without trying too hard, and it will start to take shape."

"Sounds good to me," Maggie said. "I can go for that. Let me write down this layout, so I'll have it to refer to later." She pulled a battered notebook from her bag and jotted a few notes. Then she swept the cards together with one practiced hand and replaced them on top of the deck. "I'll let you know if I come up with anything. Someone else's turn?"

When Maggie got home that night, Mike was sitting in the living-room watching the 10:00 local news from his recliner. "County commissioners," the announcer was saying, "reviewed spending by all county departments, but took no action on a resolution which would tighten controls. Our reporter, Thom

Landris, was at the Commission meeting."

Maggie walked over to Mike, gave him a peck on the side of the face, and looked up again to see the scene on the television screen shift from the news desk in the studio to the county commission chamber. "Ted," the young reporter said, "the resolution was offered by commissioner Herman Eldridge in reaction to the announcement Monday by Comptroller Sharon Thomas that certain departments had overspent for the quarter. Commissioner Eldridge said tonight he believes it is the responsibility of the commission to keep a tighter rein on spending in order to avoid a crisis at the end of the fiscal year." The table behind him was piled with stacks of computer paper.

"It's a real can of worms," Mike said, still looking at the screen. "Every level of government is pushing services and costs down to the level below—federal down to the states and states down to the local. Nobody wants to be the one to tell the citizens the bad news. As a result, local budgets are stretched so thin the departments can hardly do their job. The commissioners might as well spend their time on something other than pouring over computer print-outs.

"It's another reason not to mess with the coroner project right now," he continued. "Everybody involved—the commissioners, the courts, the police, the coroners themselves—has their hands full." He paused and turned his head away from the tv, in Maggie's direction. "Did you have a good time tonight?"

"As always," Maggie replied. "I also learned some things about Sondra and Nora Patterson that I think I wish I didn't know."

"Oh, that reminds me." Mike turned in his chair now to look directly at his wife. "The lab determined our neighbor definitely did not commit suicide—she was murdered!"

Maggie felt her mid-section contract, as though the words had struck a blow. "Shee-it! That's not good!" She sat down abruptly on the sofa. "I hate to think of that kind of thing here in our neighborhood. I thought they'd said nothing was disturbed in the house. Was she—molested?"

"No mention of it. She apparently let whoever it was into the house; there was no evidence of a break-in, they said. The coroner established the time of death as early Sunday evening."

CHAPTER 8

Wednesday night was Co-op night. Maggie had her choice of routes from home to get to the Buchanan Center, a repurposed grade school in Tennessee Town, an older and somewhat run-down residential section of Topeka. The General Store (which everyone called simply "the co-op") was housed in a lean-to off the back of the old brick building, just on the alley and conveniently adjacent to a concrete platform that acted as a loading dock for the store. Maggie arrived driving west on the one-way 12th Street, pulled into the alley, and parked down a ways away from the dock, to leave what little close parking there was for any paying customers.

She was signed up to work stocking shelves from seven to nine. She liked being in the small natural foods grocery, with its narrow aisles and sweet pungent smells of whole grain flour and fresh herbs. She also liked stocking. There was something about the physical routine of putting out the boxes of soy granules and veggie-burger mix, the jars of organic fruit juice and no-cholesterol mayonnaise, "fronting" and dusting the shelves that she found almost as good as yoga for bringing a calm serenity of mind. On a slow business night, she could get into such a quiet state that she went home quite refreshed.

This, however, was not to be one of those nights. A woman Maggie knew only as Kit was in charge of the counter crew volunteers for the evening shift. Kit was late arriving, and when she did get there she was out of sorts as well as out of breath. "Damned-shitty-mother-pig-cop!" she muttered. She was thin and pale, with dark, deep-set eyes and limp grey-brown hair, her mouth set in a permanently-bitter line. "I know he effin' well wouldn't have said that to an effin' man!"

"Said what?" Maggie asked automatically, and immediately wished she had not.

"I was a little late through a yellow light—well, okay, a red light, and he pulls me over and gives me an effin' safety lecture! I've been drivin' since before he was born. And when I was his age, we were makin' war on the pig-cops, not joining them!"

Well, that might be a bit of an exaggeration, Maggie thought. He can't have been that young! But against her better judgment, she shook her head sympathetically. "I'm sorry, Kit," she said. "Did you get a ticket?"

"Shit, yes!" Kit spat out. "And they'll probably use that against me in my case against the city!"

Maggie had started to turn away, but her curiosity was hooked now and she couldn't let that stand. "You're suing the city?" she asked, incredulous.

"You bet," Kit affirmed. "They're trying to take my house, and they're not going to get away with it!"

"The city is trying to take your house?" Maggie was doubtful.

"The Man!" Kit turned her back, clearly in no mood to make further conversation.

"Mmm-mmm," Maggie murmured in what she hoped would be taken as an appropriate tone and moved as quickly as she could toward the stock room. A glance at the work list showed her there were several cases of juice to be set out and bins to be replenished with split peas, organic oatmeal, and four kinds of beans. Hefting the big bags of bulk grains and legumes was one of Maggie's less favorite chores, so, characteristically, she started with that part.

She had just finished loading a new bag of oatmeal into the grain bin when Kit called her up front. Counter crew was short-handed, she said, so would Maggie please take over orienting a new customer? Maggie showed the short, balding man where to find and then how to bag, weigh, and price the black beans, pecan halves, and whole wheat flour he wanted. She patiently explained to him the check-out system and why it was that the peanut butter tubs were kept in the cooler while the honey barrel was not. When he seemed satisfied, she wished him well and went back to her stocking.

Andi Parrot came in with her red-headed twins, who charged up and down the aisles, poking at items on the shelves and banging the lids on the bulk food bins. One of them nudged Maggie's elbow as she pouring the last of the pinto beans into its bin. Looking around to see if anyone else had noticed, she brushed the dozen or so spilled beans under the edge of the bottom shelf and headed for the stock room to bring out the first case of juice.

A few minutes later, Maggie heard in the next aisle a soft voice with a trace of a German accent. "Now, dear, you might try this oil instead. It is canola, what used to be called 'rape-seed oil,' and it is a Kansas product."

That would be frail Buff Friedmann, a retired psychiatrist, and his wife, Helda. Buff and Helda, both now in their late seventies, were among the founding members of the Co-op and were highly respected elders to the people in Maggie's circle.

In a moment, Helda appeared around the corner of the coffee rack, followed by her husband leaning slightly on a dark wooden cane. "Oh, Maggie, how nice to see you," Helda said, holding out her arms for a hug.

"It's good to see you," Maggie replied, giving the small, white-haired woman a gentle cheek-by-cheek hug and then repeating the gesture with Buff.

"It is very disturbing about Nora Patterson," Buff said after a pause. "Did you know her, Maggie?"

"Hardly at all," Maggie said. "But everyone else seems to have."

"I think she had not been very active in matters here in town recently," Helda said, "but she was very active earlier—in the co-op, but also in the peace work, and mental health advocacy, and so on."

"You knew her fairly well?" Maggie asked, directing her question to both of the elders.

"Enough to be shocked at the idea that she would kill herself, absent diagnosis of a fatal disease," Buff said, looking Maggie directly in the eye. "I have known suicidal and suicide-prone people," he continued, his soft voice taking on a professorial tone, "and the ego structure...."

"Now, Buff," Helda hushed.

"But didn't you hear?" Maggie interrupted at almost the same moment. "They're not calling it suicide any more. According to last night's news, it's murder!"

Helda made an "ooo" shape with her delicate mouth, although no sound came out.

Buff nodded his head slowly. "Murder is disturbing. But not in this case any more so than a verdict of suicide by a person whose primary focus of aggression was very much outward, not inward. It was highly unlikely."

"Understand, my dear," Helda interposed, "the young woman was never a patient. My husband would not speak of a patient in this way."

"But you felt she was an angry or aggressive person?" Maggie pursued, thinking of the tiny, intense woman she had met.

"Everyone has aggression," Buff said. "Everyone has also anger, but some direct this outward, some inward. Judging by her behavior, I would say Nora Patterson was one clearly outward-directed in her aggression. Such people are seldom suicidal. Homicidal, perhaps, if the need arises, but not suicidal."

"Let Maggie get back to her work." Helda tugged gently at her husband's sleeve.

"This is very interesting to me," Maggie protested. "I'd like to hear some more."

"And we need to finish our shopping," Helda said firmly, starting to move away.

Buff shrugged his shoulders and raised his hand in a

gesture of resignation. "Perhaps another day, Maggie," he smiled, and turned to follow his wife.

A few minutes later, having emptied the box of apple juice, Maggie headed for the stock room, still musing about what Buff Friedmann had said. As she was pulling the step-stool into place to take down for another box, a pair of arms reached over her head. "Let me get that for you, Maggie."

"Why, thank you, Les, but, whoo! You startled me!"

"Uh, oh, sorry about that. Where did you want this?"

"Out here, please." Maggie led the way.

Leslie Stone was a tall man, his white t-shirt stretched tightly over broad but bony shoulders. He squatted down and set the box gently on the floor. He pulled out a jar of dark purple-red liquid. "100%-natural organic cranberry juice. Sixteen ounces," he announced.

"Thanks, Les," Maggie said again. "How have you been?"

Still squatting, Leslie rubbed his chin with his left palm, as though missing the short black beard Maggie knew he had recently shaved off. "Oh, uh, all right. I've been working on trying to become more assertive. It seems, uh, I can often get a goal clearly in mind, but, oh, uh, yes, when it comes to doing something about it, I, well, I don't, you know."

Maggie remained standing, hoping uncharitably that Leslie would take the hint and go on about his shopping. With his hesitant, whiny speech and constant self-analysis, he wore out his welcome more quickly than most.

"I might try this cranberry juice," Les continued in his self-absorbed way, still holding the jar and rubbing his chin again. "I'm, uh, changing my diet, you know. I was told that, uh, I was being, uh, too strict in my discipline. Well, yes, too strict. No meat, of course, and uh, no animal products at all—well, I'm still using no animal products, but, uh, I'm, well, yes, adding some fruit and some cooked vegetables. Well, beans, you know, and cooked greens when I can. It's still a discipline, but I'm, uh, trying to be, well, a bit gentler with myself.

"How about you?" he asked after a moment.

"Oh, I'm fine," Maggie said.

"Uh, quite a shock about Nora Patterson. Doesn't she live near you?"

"Yes, she did. You knew her?"

"Well, yes. I suppose everyone around here, uh, I mean, did know her, more or less. Don't you think?" Les scratched the back of his head and pursed his lips.

"So it would seem. I had only just met her myself."

"Do you know if they have any leads to who, uh, did it?"

"No, but then I wouldn't. That's up to the city police, and my husband is with the Kansas Bureau of Investigation. They don't get involved in homicide unless their help is requested—which is usually in the rural areas that have no investigators of their own." Besides which, if I did know anything "out-of-school" I'd better be darn sure I didn't tell anybody, Maggie added to herself. Being a cop's wife brought some juicy news sometimes, but also the frustration of never being able to gossip about it!

Suddenly, Maggie squatted down beside Les. "I just realized! Didn't someone tell me you and Nora rode up to Kansas City together to a workshop just last weekend? You must have known her rather well. I'm really sorry, Leslie!" She started to pick up the carton of juice and lowered it again, and put her hand comfortingly on the man's arm.

"I'm really sorry," she said again. "Are you okay?"

"Yes, well, yes, I'm okay," he said dully, staring at the fruit juice jar he still held. "Yes, well, uh, thanks." He stood. "I guess I'd better go. Goodbye, Maggie." He turned abruptly and strode toward the front of the store.

Maggie stared after him, concerned. Then she shrugged, sighed, and returned to her labors.

Before long, however, her thoughts were interrupted again, by a deep voice from the end of the aisle.

"Well, well! Maggie Tenwhistle!"

She looked up to see a blond bear of a man lumbering toward her, wearing a light-blue coverall and a broad grin.

Maggie straightened from her work and stretched out her arms. "Carl Nelson," she cried, as the man reached her and swept her off her feet in a great embrace.

When the bear set her down again, the two backed a little way apart. "How are you?" they asked in unison, and both laughed.

"I see Mike every once in a while, but—" began Carl.

"How are Alice and the boys?" started Maggie at the same time.

"You first," said Carl, after another burst of laughter from both.

"Okay. How are Alice and the boys? I haven't seen any of you for ages."

"Everyone's fine. The boys are both out for track—in fact, I just came from a meet. Ray puts the shot, and Roy throws the discus. It keeps them in shape for football. And you? I see Mike from time to time, but it's usually business."

"Well, you knew I left my job with the court?" Maggie said.

"Yes, and now you're working for a stock broker, is it?" Carl asked.

"Yes, with Blain, Towneshend, and Hannigan, in the old Fountain Building, just down the street from the police station. And Alice?"

Carl smiled. "Alice's doing great. She finishes her degree next month, and then she'll be hunting for a teaching job. She's really looking forward to it. She'll be sorry to have missed seeing you. She'd been at the track meet all afternoon, so I sent her on home. We haven't had supper yet, and I'm just here to get some of that instant refried bean stuff."

"I've never tried that. Everybody says it's really good," Maggie said. She remembered two young couples in Lindsborg, struggling to raise their babies on law enforcement officers' and secretaries' paychecks. She and Mike and Carl and Alice Nelson had encouraged each other over many a pot of beans.

"It is good, and quick. And no lard in it, unlike the canned kind," Carl said. "Even the boys like it. Well—say, I guess Mike isn't here?"

"He will be in about half an hour. He's coming by to pick me up. He had a meeting tonight at the library, and we decided we could travel in one car for a change—you know, actually carpool!" Maggie chuckled at her own wry joke.

"Okay, I probably can't wait that long. Would you ask him to give me a call when you-all get home? I need to talk to him," Carl said.

"You-*all*?" Maggie echoed. "I didn't realize you were from *southern* Lindsborg! Sure, I'll have him call you, Carl."

"I meant you all, you and he," Carl paused, flustered, his fair face flushing to the hairline. "You knew what I meant!"

"Of course I did," soothed Maggie, instantly sorry she hadn't remembered how easily embarrassed this gentle man was. "I've always thought English really needed a plural second-person pronoun, and 'you-all' is the best we have—certainly lots better to my ear than 'youse.' And I will have him call you."

"Well, I'd better get going," Carl said after an awkward pause. "Great to see you, Maggie."

"We really must get together, all of us, again soon." Maggie smiled warmly. "I don't know how it is we let old friends…oh, you know." She reached out to Carl, who this time bent his knees in an awkward but effective move to hug her face to face. "Give Alice and the boys my love," said Maggie.

"Maybe we can have a picnic one of these days," Carl said, starting to leave. He turned back and enunciated carefully: "YOU ALL could come over to our house and we could grill something."

"We-all would love it. Have Alice give me a call," Maggie replied, relieved to know she hadn't really hurt his feelings with her teasing. "See you soon, then. Bye-bye."

When Mike arrived to pick her up, Maggie had nearly

finished the last case of juice, and he helped her set out the last few jars. "If we go quickly," she whispered guiltily, "we won't have to help close up. I've worked more than my two hours anyway."

"Don't you need to buy anything?" Mike queried.

"I was going to, but I didn't have time. Too many interruptions. Let's just go. I'll go to Dillons, or do without till Saturday."

They slipped out the door with a quick goodbye to Kit on her stool by the cash register, scowling over someone else's order.

In the car, Maggie remembered to tell Mike about Carl's request that he call, and recounted the intriguing comments of Dr. Friedmann. "He hadn't heard that the coroner was calling it murder, but he'd reached essentially the same conclusion himself, just by reference to her personality," Maggie said thoughtfully.

"Did Carl say what he wanted," Mike asked.

"No, I thought you'd know."

"I expect I do. He was who I called this morning about this business with Nora, and I assume he's getting back to me."

"Oh! Can you call him tonight?"

"It's nearly 10:00 now, Tiger," Mike said. "I know your curiosity is about to get the best of you, but I think I'll wait till morning. Our Carl is an early-to-bed bird.

"Just like somebody else I know," he added, as Maggie let out a loud yawn. "Did anything else happen of interest?"

Maggie thought for a moment. "Oh, yes, I guess. Kit—you remember Kit? She's the science writer, who works the counter sometimes."

"And scares away any potential new customers because she's so rude?" Mike laughed. "Yes, I remember her!"

"Okay, well, she told me she's suing the city of Topeka," Maggie continued. "Someone is trying to take her house, and she's 'effing' not going to let them get away with it. Do you have any idea what that's about?"

"It's been covered in the news," Mike said.

"Okay, so, what's the deal?" Maggie queried. "You know I don't have time to read the local news."

"Well, to put it briefly, you know her house is on a strip of land between the Foundation campus and the Governor's mansion. Right?"

"Uh-huh," Maggie nodded.

"And a contractor has been wanting to buy the land from the Foundation and put in luxury condos. The planning commission approved the necessary change in zoning, and the commission accepted it. As a renter, Kit has no real say in the matter, but she's suing the city, trying to stop the project so she doesn't lose her home."

"Huh! As far as I know, she's a throughly disagreeable person," Maggie mused. "But I hate to see anyone lose their home. Is she going to have any chance of overturning it?"

"I doubt it," Mike said. "The case will be coming up for trial soon. But there's nothing you can do to help," he added, frowning a little and shaking his head. "Please tell me you won't try."

Maggie yawned again, stretching her arms carefully so as not to interfere with Mike, as he turned into their driveway. "I'll probably forget it as soon as I get in the house," she said drowsily.

CHAPTER 9

The next morning dawned gray and thundery. When the alarm went off, Maggie groaned and pulled the covers up over her head. "Could we just pretend we're both sick today?" she asked hopefully.

"Nope, nope, nope!" Mike pronounced briskly, yanking the covers away from his wife. "I have lots to do today, and if I have to get up, you have to get up!"

"You're a big meanie, you know," Maggie grumbled, but she got up and tossed the sheet toward the pillows in a half-hearted effort to spread up the bed. "Oh, don't forget to call Carl. Could you call him from home, so I'd get to hear what he has to say?"

"You know what that attitude did to poor pussy," Mike teased.

"Okay, so don't make me wait any longer than necessary."

"I'll see about it," Mike promised. "Now let me go get the paper."

As they were sitting down to breakfast, the rain began. Light but steady at first, then harder, until it was coming down in torrents. Maggie peeled a banana and began slicing it onto her Cheerios. "I had a strange dream last night," she said thoughtfully. "This morning, really. I can't remember what came before or after, but there was a loud bang, like an explosion or maybe a shot, and a shattered glass bowl, a fruit bowl, because there were smashed-up apples and grapes and oranges tumbling all over the ground. And it seems like it was snowing, or everything was covered with snow or something." She closed her eyes and willed the misty threads of the dream to reshape themselves into something meaningful. Which, of course, they did not.

Just as Maggie was spooning up the last of her cereal, the phone rang. While Maggie answered the kitchen phone, Mike left the table and headed toward the living room to finish the morning paper.

"That was Sondra," she called to him when she hung up the phone. "She was confirming that the Pattersons want me to house sit for them during the memorial service this morning."

"At Orin Patterson's house?"

"No, just up the street, at Nora's. There's been some trouble with people coming around, curious and such, even with family members staying in the house, and they don't want to leave it empty during the service," Maggie explained. "I've already told the office I wouldn't be in today, just in case. If I wasn't going to do this, I'd told Sondra I'd go with her to the service."

Maggie ran water in the sink and started to wash the breakfast dishes. Then she pursed her lips and put the cup she was washing back in the water. Drying her soapy hands, she walked into the living room. "I don't like to nag, Mike, but are you going to call Carl?"

"In a minute, Maggie."

"Okay, but just please do it before he leaves for work?"

"Trust me."

Maggie shrugged and headed back toward the kitchen, still holding the towel. "This is kind of important to me," she said over her shoulder.

Mike folded his paper and reached for the phone at his elbow. Maggie heard him greet Carl, but after she went upstairs to get ready to leave she heard nothing more of the conversation. A few minutes later, as she stood before the bathroom mirror slipping on her favorite pair of rose-quartz earrings, Mike reappeared, his face unusually sober.

"Well? What?" Maggie demanded. "You look—solemn."

"I don't know any good way to say this, Tiger," Mike

began. "Nora Patterson was murdered by someone she knew and trusted. Someone who had a key to her house. She hadn't just let some stranger in. The front and back doors were left bolted, and the garage door was down. No sign of any struggle, no keys missing."

Maggie took a deep breath, but said nothing.

"She was found sitting in a chair in the dining room, although she'd already cleaned up after the meal, which according to the stomach contents she'd eaten about an hour earlier. She was dressed for bed, Carl said, and her own gun was on the floor beside her. They brought up a couple of her prints on the weapon—" Maggie shot Mike an interrogatory glance. "and no others. Which, together with the single gunshot wound to the chest, would have tended to confirm the first assumption that the victim had committed suicide."

"But you said—" Maggie began.

"Maggie, somebody deliberately, cold-bloodedly, tried to make it look like suicide. But he or she wasn't very skillful. From the lack of powder on either the victim's hands or her chest, she clearly didn't shoot herself." Mike paused, looking intently at Maggie.

"And?"

"Sondra is a prime suspect."

"Why?" Maggie was aware that she had been staring wide-eyed and open-mouthed for the past several moments. "Why would they suspect Sondra?"

"Why not? She admits she had a key to the house, she lives right next door, the victim had wrecked her marriage—motive, means (she could easily have known where Nora kept her gun), and opportunity." Mike spoke in an unemotional tone that was at odds with the very real concern his face betrayed.

"Carl really wanted me to advise you that you should be very careful. Sondra is a suspect. If she is involved, you could get into real trouble poking around."

"But she's my friend!" Maggie protested. "Besides, what do you mean, poking around?"

"Don't play coy with me, Maggie," Mike said seriously. "I know when the cat's curiosity is aroused. And this is nothing to fool with. Just leave it alone, stay away from Sondra, and don't give her or anyone else reason to feel threatened by you."

"I don't know that I can stay away from Sondra," Maggie said, thinking. "I've already promised to stay at the Patterson house, and I...not that I think for a minute that she had anything to do with this! But if she did, she'd think something was odd for sure if I started ignoring her all of a sudden." She broke off, her mind racing.

"Just be careful," Mike said with a sigh. "They've talked to her, and her answers are 'not entirely satisfactory.'" He made the finger quotes. "I have to go." He leaned over to kiss her. "I love you."

"I love you, too," Maggie returned absently.

As Mike headed out the door, Maggie was busily mulling over the few facts she knew about what she had started to think of as "the case." It was disturbingly clear that Sondra could be imagined to have an obvious motive for hating Nora, as well as the opportunity to have done the deed.

But she couldn't have! Maggie shook her head firmly. So the next question was, who could have? Somebody else with a key, according to the police. So—that could be the daughters, Kara and Karin (maybe Karin was out, as living too far away?), Orin? (maybe), other close friends, current lovers, maybe past lovers, too. Maggie realized she didn't know enough about Nora to even begin to speculate, and told herself resolutely to drop the subject.

An hour and a half later, umbrella in hand, Maggie stood on the step in front of Nora Patterson's door, looking toward the street through the dense evergreen trees. Pretty hard for curiosity-seekers to see anything without coming up the drive, she thought. Also, pretty hard for any neighbors to see who came and went. Except for Sondra, who had a more or less unobstructed view from her front door if she happened to be looking. Maggie shivered, not entirely from the damp chill. Maybe she should leave the detecting to the city officers—but she couldn't seem to stop wondering.

She rang the bell and the door was opened almost immediately by Orin Patterson, who invited her in and introduced her to the extended family gathered within—his parents, Nora's mother, and his wife, Lorraine.

"Oh, but we've met," Maggie said when introduced to the latter. "Monday night?"

"Yes, of course," said Lorraine, sounding uncertain. "I'm sorry, I've met so many people since…."

"I'm sure," Maggie soothed quickly. "And at such a difficult time for all of you." Especially difficult for the second wife of the deceased's ex, she thought. Wonder how she and Nora got along.

Orin's father was slender, like his son, and very straight, though age had silvered his hair and, Maggie surmised, probably shortened him an inch or two. The elder Mrs. Patterson was small and white-haired, but obviously still full of protective concern for her son, whom she now took aside for a whispered conference.

Nora's mother, a Mrs. Finnan, was also petite and white-haired, but the burden of time, and perhaps of this latest sorrow, had bent and wrung her so that she had a profound "dowager's hump" and raised her head to look Maggie in the face only with difficulty.

"You're a friend of Nora's?" she asked, a note in her voice that Maggie would under other circumstances have termed "wistful."

"An acquaintance, really. I live down the street. I've come to stay at the house during the service. You know, be sure nobody bothers it," she said.

"Nora's house," the woman replied in a flat voice. She did not seem to expect an answer, as she stared at the floor.

"I'm very sorry for your loss," Maggie said, wishing for Mrs. Finnan's sake that she had been closer to Nora so she could say something more personal.

"People are still bringing food," Kara Patterson said, coming up to her grandmother's side. "We've had more than we can really use. Mother's friends and neighbors have been so kind."

"People want to help," Maggie said. It sounded trite, even to her, and she wondered how much of the "help" in this case was motivated at least in part by morbid curiosity.

"Mother Finnan." Orin Patterson spoke from across the room. "It's time we were going. Would you like to ride with Karin and Kara, and Mom and Pop can ride with Lorraine and me?"

Coming up to offer the older woman his arm, he spoke in an aside to Maggie. "I appreciate your staying while we're gone. Unfortunately, I feel there is a need for someone to be here. Karin and Kara have been staying here with their grandmother and we've had some strange visitors even with the house occupied. Just don't open the door to anyone you don't know."

"I'm happy to do it," Maggie said. "Please don't think any more about it. I'll be here until you get back, so there's no need to worry."

"Will you be going out this way?" she continued, reaching for the door that led to the garage.

"Yes, Karin has been using Nora's car," Orin explained, leading Mrs. Finnan down the steps from the kitchen into the attached two-car garage.

"Mine's such a jalopy, Karin wouldn't be caught dead in it," Kara said cheerfully. If she noticed the inappropriateness of her phrase, she didn't show it, as she pretended to poke an elbow into the ribs of her older sister who had silently joined the procession toward the garaged car.

"Kara, open the garage, will you?" Karin requested, swinging the driver's side door wide and settling behind the wheel, as her father helped her grandmother into the front passenger seat.

"Oh, this one doesn't work," Kara said, pointing to a small

button on the wall near where Maggie stood. "It hasn't worked for months. You'll have to use the one in the car." Karin had already closed the car door and appeared not to have heard, so Kara repeated the information in pantomime, shaking her head in a vigorous negative while pointing to the wall button, and then gesturing toward her sister and the car with several jabs of a finger while nodding meaningfully.

Karin seemed to get the message, for she raised her right hand toward the sun visor, then leaned back and started the car. The garage door slid silently upward, dripping water on the garage floor and stopping with a soft thud. As Kara climbed into the back seat of the car, behind her sister, Orin strode out into the rain and down the driveway to join his parents and wife in the maroon Buick Maggie remembered seeing there earlier in the week. She wondered idly why he hadn't pulled into the empty second half of the garage. Maybe they'd arrived before the rain started.

Maggie watched both cars drive away until her view was blocked as the garage door closed, presumably in response to a signal from an electronic gizmo inside Nora's car. As she went back into the kitchen, Maggie wondered, not for the first time, how people got their cars out if the electronics failed altogether —as in her experience electronics invariably did sooner or later.

CHAPTER 10

Alone in the empty house, Maggie found herself at a loss for something to do. She wandered from the kitchen into the dining room and stood looking at the oval dining table and its matching reddish-brown chairs (maple, she guessed). She trailed her finger idly across the polished tabletop and then sniffed. Smelled fresh. "Lemon Pledge," perhaps, but not having used any furniture polish herself for years, Maggie couldn't be sure.

She pulled aside blue-green drapes to reveal a sliding glass door leading to a small brick patio and the back yard. Although the grass wasn't showing much sign of green, flower buds on a large maple tree were swollen red with springtime enthusiasm. Orderly raised garden beds, now shiny with standing water, showed signs of recent cultivation. A wood and wire structure Maggie identified as a fancy compost box stood near the alley at the back of the lot, beside it a large pile of dead leaves.

Nora must have been doing lots of cleaning up in the last few weeks, getting ready for spring planting, Maggie thought. How ironic! But on the other hand, perhaps it was a blessing to have death catch you unaware, doing your regular thing, living your life. Probably made a difference whether you were ready to die. "Live every day as though it would be your last" was good advice, she'd often thought—at least for people who didn't have small children depending on them.

The doorbell buzzed, breaking into Maggie's reverie. When she looked through the narrow glass panel beside the front door, she saw Suzanne and Anna huddled together under a huge maroon umbrella.

"Hello, you two," she said, throwing the door open. "What are you doing out in this rain?"

"We're on our way to the memorial service. What are you doing here?" Suzanne asked, motioning Anna to precede her in the door.

"I volunteered to house-sit. Or at least, Sondra volunteered me, and I was glad to do it. I didn't know Nora well enough to need go to the service, but I'm happy for a way to help, anyway."

"We brought lasagna," Anna said, holding out a large aluminum pan. "Do they have lots of food already?"

"I think they do, but we can put this in the freezer. Do you need the pan back?" Maggie said, reaching for it.

"Nope. Learned that lesson from my dad's death," Anna replied. "People bringing food to the bereaved is a fine old tradition—"

"Comforting in a very primitive way," Suz interjected.

"But getting all the dishes returned afterward is a real bitch!" Anna finished.

"I suppose it would be," Maggie said. "I never thought about that from the family's point of view. Do you guys have time to come in?"

"Not really," Suz said, looking at her watch. "We need to be going. Are you doing okay?"

"Me? Oh, I'm fine," Maggie assured her. "I'm a bit concerned about Sondra, of course, and, well, the whole thing is…"

"Not too comfortable, is it? I know. Me, too," Anna said.

"We were just talking about it on the way over here," Suz continued. "Nora was a—shall we say she had a strong personality, but it's hard to imagine…" She glanced at her watch again. "We really do have to go, but are you doing anything for lunch? Could we pick you up after the service?"

"I don't know what time I'll be through here. But, yes, that would be great if you don't mind…I have to wait till they get back, you know."

"Anna?"

"I'm not working today. And you?"

"I don't have any clients this afternoon, and I can just call in and tell the office 'I have been delayed.'" Suz lifted her chin and gestured imperiously with her left hand.

"Must be nice to be a rich lawyer," Anna said *sotto voce* to Maggie. "Of course, you're going to become a rich stock broker and then I'll be the only poor one."

"I'm not so sure I'm going to make it," Maggie said. "Time will tell. So, you'll stop by when you're done, and we'll leave for lunch as soon as the family gets back? I'll tell them you were by."

"Yeah, we have to get going," Suz repeated. "See you soon."

As the tall woman struggled getting her umbrella's nearly-four-foot length through the door, Maggie teased, "Think you've got a big enough 'brolly?"

"Yes, well, it's Will's golf umbrella, but it does good on a day like this," Suz replied, raising the now-open umbrella to shelter both herself and Anna.

"Bye now." Maggie closed the door behind her friends, and turned toward the kitchen.

She set the foil-covered dish on the counter and raised the lid of the freezer. Plenty of room, she thought, as she set the lasagna into a nearly-empty basket. A surprising amount of room, considering the freezer had been almost too full to accommodate Yertle—was it just barely over a week ago? How could Nora have emptied out her freezer so fast? Or had the family? You wouldn't have thought they'd be so organized as to have started moving things out already.

Maggie closed the lid and stood staring at the chest. Come to think of it, hadn't Sondra said the turtle was in the bottom of the freezer when she came to pick him up the day after Nora…? People did odd things in grief, but why would you clear out a person's freezer before they were even in the ground?

Suddenly determined to snoop while she had the chance, Maggie walked over to the telephone stand with its cluttered cork-board and began reading the notes and clippings.

As she thumbed through the overlapping items pinned to the board, a shiver of well-bred guilt ran up her spine. I'm doing it for Sondra, she told herself firmly. If I'm going to find out who else could have killed Nora, I have to know more about her. A coupon for "Lemon-lite Detoxification Supplement," a newspaper clipping announcing the opening of a new art gallery, a yellowed flier from a curb-side recycling entrepreneur, an invitation to a N.O.W. rally—not very exciting, Maggie thought.

The next item she uncovered was more interesting. For starters, the paper was mauve (at least she thought so, never having been sure just what color "mauve" was). "Catch the Light!" it proclaimed in large type above a Xeroxed photo of a balding Caucasian man with protruding eyes and a slight smile. "Baba Sin De facilitates your growth by opening your consciousness to perceptions you only dreamed of. Ph.D., D.D., R.M.T." The poster gave a meeting location in a Unity church in Kansas City, and two events, a "free lecture" on Friday, November 17, and a "two-day Enlightenment Encounter" on Saturday and Sunday, November 18-19. "For information," a phone number with a Kansas City area code was listed.

Now she was getting somewhere, Maggie exulted. This sounded like the guy Nora had gone to K.C. to see. She tore off the top sheet of the phone pad and copied the name "Baba Sin De," the address, and the phone number. Then a short hand-written list of names and phone numbers caught her eye: Les —256-2261; Pat—232-8889; Kathy—913-299-7171; Harrison—267-4517. Two local numbers, one probably rural Shawnee County, and one maybe Kansas City, Kansas, she guessed. One or two or three women, one or two or three men, depending on which gender Pat and Les turned out to be.

Before she could think better of it, Maggie snatched the note off the board and stuck it in her pocket, along with the notes about Baba Whoever. She'd better snoop fast, she told herself, if she was going to do any good.

Motive is important, she thought, moving through the hall into the living room. And to figure out motive, it helps to know the victim. Maggie strolled into the living room and looked around. The sofa and matching chairs were upholstered in crushed velvet of a light blue-gray which picked up the same shade in the figured carpet. Heavy cream-colored drapes matched another accent in the carpet, which was predominantly navy, red, and gold.

Except for photos above the fireplace, the room seemed surprisingly sterile. Tasteful, clean, and almost totally absent the usual touches that "make a house a home." Apparently it was more a formal parlor than a room Nora had lived in to any significant extent. Maggie wondered whether it might have been decorated to entertain clients (or others who needed to be impressed) in the days before Orin moved out.

Maggie walked to the end of the room to examine the framed photos arranged on the mantel. They looked to be high school graduation portraits of both Karin and Kara, Karin's "capping" photo, and a couple of family candids, one showing a young Orin at a lakeside somewhere, tall and thin, with a preschool Kara on his shoulders and a chest-high Karin standing proudly in front, all of them grinning widely.

The other snap was of the two girls at about twelve and sixteen, standing stiffly on either side of a bare-branched tree with leaf rakes in hand. Both were looking warily at a pile of leaves in front of them. Maggie picked up the photo and on closer examination realized that what she had taken for an unusually large leaf in the center of the pile was actually the top of Nora's head, with just her eyes and nose emerging below. The Midwestern version of covering Momma with sand at the beach, Maggie surmised, although the girls' ages and their expressions suggested that the game had not been entirely spontaneous, at least on their part.

Suddenly eager to move out of this room, Maggie climbed the stairs leading to the second story. On her immediate right, she found a bathroom, done up in bright rose and white and lavender, pretty in a dramatic, flowery sort of way. Nothing in the medicine cabinet or linen closet seemed exceptional, although Maggie did note the half-used package of birth control pills on the shelf over the stool. Nora's? she wondered. If she'd been still on the pill at her age, she must have found a very lenient gynecologist. Not that it mattered now. Maggie shrugged. More likely belonged to one of the girls. Things were so much more open these days!

One bedroom was obviously being used by Mrs. Finnan. Maggie took a quick look around, but saw nothing of interest. Another bedroom, with twin beds, was just as clearly where Kara and Karin were sleeping, and from the posters on the walls and the stuffed animals in one corner had probably been Kara's room before she moved into her own apartment. Somehow, Maggie didn't feel like looking through suitcases. She wasn't sure whether it was proper breeding that held her back or a fear of being caught (which could have stemmed from too many spy stories where the hero laid a hair across the lid of whatever he didn't want opened).

She moved on to the largest bedroom, which had to be Nora's. A king-sized bed with a royal purple velvet spread dominated the room. White shag carpet (of a depth Maggie doubted could be purchased anymore) covered the floor as well as a window seat along the far wall. A faded red rose on the bed-side table had dropped all but a few petals, and no one had cleaned them up. Not surprising, Maggie supposed. Probably no one had been in the room much in the past few days.

She looked into the closet. Nothing especially striking—a few skirts, a few t-shirts and blouses, a basket of laundry on the floor. Maggie closed the closet door, experiencing not for the first time the sad sense of futility which the intimate belongings of the dead arouse in the living.

She moved briskly to the large bookcase which covered one wall, and began reading titles: A *Place of Power, The Vision of Sri Baba Yong, Living on Light: A Dietary Miracle.* She skimmed several more shelves: *Organic Gardening Now, A Workbook for Non-violent Conflict Resolution, Animal Slavery: the Dread Comparison*—nothing surprising. *The Kama Sutra, Tantric Sex for Western Lovers, Sexual Ecstasy: a Handbook*—Maggie pulled that one off the shelf. The cover had a drawing of a vaguely Asian-looking couple, standing facing each other, palms touching, while their auras blazed and blended in a spectacular rainbow of colors.

Looks like fun, Maggie thought, and began to leaf through the book. She skimmed chapter titles: "Yin and Yang," "Energy Flow and Opening to Love," "The Psychology of Letting Go." There were diagrams of the human body, male and female, with arrows showing the directions of energy flow, and sketches of couples connected in various positions, with arrows showing—the doorbell interrupted her browsing. Darn! Just as it was getting interesting!

Maggie jammed the book back on the shelf, ran lightly down the stairs, and hurried to answer the door. It was Suz and Anna. As it turned out, the Pattersons drove up just moments later. Maggie, feeling only a bit guilty, accepted the thanks of Orin Patterson, and after murmuring further condolences, she and her friends were on their way to lunch.

"So were there lots of people there?" Maggie asked eagerly, as soon as they were away from the curb. "I started to say 'Was there a good turnout?' but I guess that's not too appropriate."

"I'd say 'turnout' would be okay in this instance," Suz commented drily. "Just about everyone and his or her dog showed up, including a couple of cops."

"Well, they always do that in the movies," Maggie said. "Show up at the funeral, looking for suspects."

"They'd have had a hard time sorting anyone out of this crowd," Suz said. "The Fellowship auditorium was packed, and people were standing in the kitchen, the classrooms, and the hallway."

"Oh, the service was at the Fellowship?" Maggie asked, surprised. "I didn't know Nora was a Unitarian."

"She wasn't a member," Anna replied. "But that's a place she and Orin had attended at one time, and I guess the family felt comfortable with it."

"In this kind of weather, it was better than holding the service in the city park or out by the river bank, which would have been more Nora's style," Suz added.

"Well, what kind of a service was it?" Maggie probed, thinking that if she were a real detective, she should have gone to the service instead of house-sitting.

"Very informal, as you can imagine," Anna began. "The minister stood up and said a few words at the beginning, and then invited whoever had something to offer to come up and say or sing or play it."

"And they did!" Suz continued. "Each of the girls—Kara and Karin—came up and laid a yellow rose on the coffin. Les Stone tried to read a poem, but got so choked up he couldn't continue."

"Kathy Gegeshina, from Kansas City, sang a couple of songs. Do you know her?" Anna asked, turning around to look at Maggie in the back seat.

"What's the name? I don't think so," Maggie said.

"Kathy Gegeshina," Suz said. "You watch the road, Anna. I'll explain. Kathy used to lead the Sufi dancing when that was happening regularly in Lawrence. There were a half-dozen or so who went over for that once a month. Nora and Orin, Sondi, sometimes Sam, and some of the rest of us from time to time."

"Anyway," Anna resumed, as she pulled into the restaurant parking lot, "Kathy sang, and a young man, who seemed to be with Sondi and Jas, played the guitar and sang a song he said he had written especially for the occasion."

"Actually, he said he had written it for Nora." Suz opened her door. "It was lovely—something about her 'bright spirit, loving heart,' a really touching, melancholy song."

THE CORONER HAD NO COMMENT

Over lunch, the conversation moved on to other topics. As Anna was driving her home, Maggie returned to the discussion of the memorial service. "Did you say this woman who sang was from Kansas City?" she asked.

"Kathy? Yes, she used to live in Lawrence, but she's been in KC for years now." Anna pulled into Maggie's driveway. "You may not have ever met her."

"Maybe not. I wonder if she is in this group Nora was going to in Kansas City. The one she went to that last weekend."

"Could be. I can try to find out, if you like."

"I think I know who to ask," Maggie said. "Thanks."

CHAPTER 11

As Maggie opened her front door, the phone was ringing. "Oh, shoot!" she muttered under her breath, juggling handbag, keys, and umbrella while trying to close the door behind her. As the phone continued its insistent call, she dropped everything on the landing and half-stumbled, half-jumped down the three steps and into the kitchen, where she grabbed the phone off the hook. After pausing a moment to breathe, she managed a gracious "Hello?"

"Maggie. It's Sondra. I need your help."

"Sondra?" Maggie sighed (inaudibly, she hoped), and then said brightly, "Sure, if I can. What is it?"

"I need to talk to you, and my house is flooding. I've got Leslie and Kara and the Friedmanns and some other people coming anyway—I was going to have an Equinox ritual—and I'm calling some more, but I thought if you could come too, or Geoffrey or both, or whatever—I've got to get the carpet up, and that means carrying some things upstairs, and the more people, the better. Just if you can, of course. If you can't, I understand. But it would really help, and I do need to talk to you anyway!"

"Oh, of course, Sondra. Let me change my clothes, and check my own patio drain. Unless I have problems of my own, I'll be right down."

When Maggie peered out at her own patio, the drain seemed to be going fine. She shrugged out of her coat, and hung it over a kitchen chair to drip, then headed upstairs to change.

"O-o-o-oh, i-i-it ain't gonna rain no more, no more," she sang loudly. "It ain't gonna rain no more. But how in the heck can

I wash my neck, if it ain't-a gonna rain no more?" She stripped off damp slacks and blouse and rummaged in the closet for an old sweatshirt and a pair of well-worn jeans.

"It ain't gonna rain no more, no more." The next line was muffled, as she pulled the sweatshirt over her head. "But how in the hell can the old folks tell that it ain't-a gonna rain no more?"

Sondra's house, she knew, was situated so that the neighbor's yards on three sides drained toward hers. Even an expensive tiling job had apparently not taken care of the problem there. What a mess! Maggie thought. Poor Sondra.

Sondra! "I need to talk to you," she had said. Maggie realized with a start that she had completely forgotten Sondra's bigger problem. What was a little water in your house compared with being chief suspect in a murder case! Did Sondra realize? Suddenly Maggie was much more interested in seeing Sondra than she had been when it was only a question of a wet carpet.

Grabbing her coat from the kitchen and the umbrella and handbag from the landing where she'd dropped them, Maggie flipped the lock and slammed the door behind her. My shoes are already soaked, might as well walk, she thought. The rain seemed to be letting up as she splashed her way down the street. Maybe they'd get some relief soon. Spring showers, okay, but enough was enough. Whatever happened to sunny Kansas?

When Maggie arrived at Sondra's, she found the front door ajar. She pushed it open, to find a scene of what seemed to be purposeful chaos. Furniture was sitting at odd angles, wet rags and towels lay here and there on the floor. A dark stain on the edge of the living room carpet marked how far the water had encroached.

"Hi, Maggie!" Sondra appeared from behind a china cabinet in the living room. She was barefoot, jeans rolled up to her knees, a red bandanna holding her hair back.

"We're just carrying everything we can upstairs. The heavier pieces we'll pick up when we're ready to roll up the rug. You could help empty that bookcase, if you want to. Orin and Jas were just starting to carry the books upstairs, and with a few more people, you could organize a chain."

Maggie quickly found herself in the center of a fire brigade type operation, receiving stacks of books from Orin Patterson a few steps below her and handing them on to a broad-shouldered, dark-haired youth in tight jeans who swung the heavy volumes up to Kara Patterson with an ease Maggie envied.

"I'm Maggie," she said, glancing up as she passed on a couple of volumes of *The Story of Civilization*.

"Jas," the young man said. His dark eyes held hers for a moment, and Maggie decided she liked him in spite of the dirty look of his two-day beard.

"This could really build my muscles if I did it regularly," she said, turning back to take another stack of books from Orin.

"Yes," Orin said, smiling up at her.

His rather snug t-shirt did nothing to disguise his own well-shaped biceps, and Maggie felt a little thrill of excitement. The scenery was actually quite pleasant whether she looked up or down. Trying to think of a way to make conversation, she heaved the books upward.

"Whew! Maybe just a bit smaller stacks, if you don't mind," she suggested, after one of the books almost slipped from her rapidly-tiring hands.

"We can stop for a minute, if you like," Orin said, an expression of concern coming over his handsome face.

"Oh, no, I think I'm okay. Just maybe not quite such heavy stacks." God! Now he's going to think I'm a real pansy, she complained to herself. "How are things going with you, Orin?" she said, hoping to change the subject.

"Not bad," he replied. "Of course, this business with Nora's death is upsetting," he continued, lowering his voice and looking sideways at Kara, who appeared to be lost in her own thoughts, mechanically stacking books at the top of the stairs. "We feel they've made a mistake in ruling it a murder. With no way for anyone to have gotten in or out of the house, we've resigned ourselves that, for whatever reason, Nora must have taken her own life. It's hard to believe, but…it's really the only explanation that makes sense."

Actually, not the only explanation, Maggie thought. "Hmmm," she murmured, nodding sympathetically. "I understand the service was very nice," she said, suddenly uncomfortable as questions crowded her mind, none of which she could very well ask Orin right now.

"Yes, very nice," Orin said. "And thank you again for your help, keeping an eye on the house."

"I was glad to do it," Maggie said. "Are you here for the Equinox ritual, Jas?" she continued, swinging around to pass more books.

"Oh! Well, yes." The young man seemed caught off-guard by the question. "Yes, I guess that happens after we rescue the carpet and dry things out a bit. Are you staying for that?"

"I don't think so," Maggie replied, remembering how long such things usually took at Sondra's house. "I have a husband and kid at home who will expect supper after a while."

"Well, this is the last of the books," Orin spoke from below. "Jas, want to help me carry the bookcase upstairs?"

"I'll help Kara move the rest of the books out of the way up here," Maggie volunteered, as she and Jas squeezed past each other on the stairs.

"Is Jas a friend of yours?" she asked Kara confidentially, as they carried the remaining books into Sondra's bedroom.

"Not really," Kara replied, shaking her head.

"No?" Maggie was surprised.

"Actually, he's a friend of Sondra's," Kara said shortly.

Wonder what that's about, Maggie thought. She had no time to ponder, however, as Orin and Jas came into the room carrying the empty bookcase, followed by a slender young man with reddish-blond hair and a short red beard, carrying a large Oriental vase.

"Where should I put this?" the young man asked.

"You can put it up your…" Kara cried hoarsely, her voice trailing off as she rushed out of the room and down the stairs.

The two younger men looked at each other. Orin frowned and began to set down his end of the bookcase. Not having much choice, Jas followed suit. Maggie covered her confusion by advising the blond young man on where to set his breakable burden, even though it appeared obvious that no place in the cluttered room was going to be truly out of harm's way.

Back downstairs once more, Maggie looked for Sondra and found her squeezing out towels that had been holding back the water still seeping in around the back door. "Want some help there?" Maggie inquired.

"No, I'm done here for now," Sondra replied, stuffing the last wrung-out towel back in front of the door. "I think we're just about ready to move the rug. And now that the rain seems to have stopped, we can take it out back and hang it over the fence to dry out."

Maggie walked into the living room, now almost cleared of furniture, where Orin and Jas were debating whether or how to move a large over-stuffed chair. She looked out the front window to see that, in the abrupt way of Kansas weather, the rain had indeed stopped, and a warm sun was drying things out so quickly that the street in front of the house seemed to be steaming. She stared at the shimmery brightness and replayed in her mind the scene that had just taken place upstairs. What could account for Kara's sullen reaction when asked about Jas and the even stranger behavior that followed?

"Hello, Maggie." Les Stone stepped from behind the door to Sondra's study and stood looking at Maggie, flexing a long piece of stout cord in his hands.

"Les! I didn't see you there. Whoo! You gave me a start." Maggie took a deep breath and tried to calm her pounding heart.

"I didn't mean to startle you. I, uh, saw you standing there, and, well, uh, would you...uh, like to, uh, help me tie up...I mean, uh..." Les held up the cord.

"What?" Maggie peered past him into the study, where a large cardboard box stood on the floor. "Oh, certainly," she said with relief as the commonsensical explanation fell into place.

As the two of them knelt on the floor to wrap the cord around the box, Maggie collected herself enough to remember she'd been going to ask Les about Kathy Gegeshina and the Kansas City group. "Last weekend—" she began.

Les looked up. "What about last weekend?"

"When you and Nora went to Kansas City—I'm sorry to bring up painful memories—but did you go to this group often? Did you and Nora go together?"

"Together? Oh, uh, yes, well, quite often…I did, and Nora, well, yes, regularly, I guess I'd say. We sometimes car-pooled, not always. Sometimes, uh, her daughter went, uh, well, and other people. Uh, yes, Baba Sin De was in town about once a month."

"What is he like?" Maggie asked, putting her finger on the knot Les had tied.

Briskly pulling the cord into a second knot, Les replied, "He's an enlightened being," as though that explained everything.

"Oh." Maggie couldn't think of anything else to say.

"Are you staying for the ritual?" Les asked, starting to wrap a second piece of cord around the box.

"I don't think so. I need to get home; my family will be home for supper," Maggie said. "And you?"

"I, uh, may stay for the ritual, but I, uh, won't, you know, eat here," Les continued, his words coming in arrhythmic spurts that reminded Maggie of the coughs and sputters of a badly out-of-tune car. "Uh, Sondra, you know, talks a lot about eating, uh, eating healthy foods, but she doesn't really, you know. I don't like being around things I'm not, uh, not supposed to, trying not to eat." He nodded for Maggie to hold the cord down for another knot. "Friends, you know, real friends don't put temptation in your way. People who say they are trying to live a pure life, and then don't—" He pulled the knot tight so quickly Maggie almost didn't get her finger out in time.

Without looking up, Les lifted the box from the floor and

stood, all in one motion. "I'll take this out to the garage," he said. Maggie was left sitting on the floor, wondering if people were always so touchy when someone near them had been brutally murdered.

"Oh, Les?" She suddenly remembered why she had brought up the Kansas City trip in the first place, and jumped up to follow him. "Les, do you know Kathy Gegeshina? Is she part of this group in Kansas City, that meets with Baba Sin De?"

"Of course," Les replied, from the front door. "Most of the meetings are at her house." He turned abruptly and disappeared outside.

"Want to help us with this carpet, Maggie?" Orin and Jas stood over a rolled-up carpet. "Sondra wants it taken outside."

"Sure," Maggie said. "Do you want me to help carry, or open doors?"

"Maybe the door," Orin said. He and Jas swung the carpet up on their shoulders, and Maggie ran ahead to open the back door. It took some doing, as she had first to remove several soaked towels from the floor in front of the door. Following the men outside, she saw that the middle of the carpet roll was sagging dramatically. She slipped in between the two and heaved upward with both hands. "This is really heavy!" she said.

"Yup," Jas grunted. "Where are we going with it?"

"If we unroll it over the back fence, it will dry out, won't it?" Maggie said hopefully.

"I expect so," Orin agreed, sloshing through standing water, "and it surely will have a better chance there than anywhere else out here."

"Can you balance it on the fence and let me help unroll it without getting it on the ground?" Maggie asked, as they reached the fence between Sondra's yard and the alley at the back of the property.

They carefully unrolled the carpet, and then stood back, looking at their handiwork. "I hope the backing doesn't crack," Jas said. "We'll have to remember that it's out here, and get it in as soon as things are dried out in there." The smallest branches of the elm and oak trees lining the alley moved ever so slightly in the light breeze.

As they turned to go back toward the house, Maggie glanced over the side fence toward what she still thought of as Nora's house. She wondered what Orin was planning to do with it—and then corrected herself. Presumably the two girls would be Nora's heirs, so any involvement Orin might have would depend on whether his daughters sought his advice.

As her gaze swept slowly over the now sun-lit yard with its soggy garden beds, her eye was caught by what looked like a thick layer of white paper or plastic a few inches below the top of Nora's compost pile. It was a white-white, not newspaper white. Odd! She started to walk toward the fence separating the two yards, her eyes fixed on the unusual-looking compost. Below the white "whatever" was two feet or so of ordinary-looking mushed down partially-decayed yard waste, and on top was six inches of what appeared to be last year's dead leaves. But what—

"Maggie?" Orin interrupted her thought, and she turned away from the fence. "Maggie, I've been wanting to ask you—you're active in the co-op, aren't you?"

"Yes, I mean, I work my stint every month," Maggie replied, catching up with Orin, who had walked on toward the house. "I'm not a member of the board or anything." She wondered what this was leading to.

"Well, you may not be the one to answer my question, then, but you can tell me who I need to talk to. I was just wanting to see whether Nora had left any unpaid bills with the co-op. I'm her executor, and I don't want to leave anything hanging."

"I think you could find out from the manager. That's Sarah Barnes, and she's at the store any time it's open. It's a paid position now, you know," Maggie said.

"No, I didn't realize that," Orin said. "Our little co-op is coming up in the world. Nora and I were founding members. Did you know that?" He opened the door for Maggie, who slipped off her thoroughly-muddy shoes before stepping inside.

"So you're not a member anymore?" Maggie turned to ask Orin, only to find that he had already walked down the short hall and was talking to Kara by the front door. Humph! Obviously he wasn't still a member, or he'd have known the co-op also didn't extend credit anymore.

"Oh, Maggie, dear. Look, Buff, it's Maggie Tenwhistle." From the kitchen came Helda Friedmann, followed by her husband.

"Hello," said Maggie, a bit distractedly. She was still holding her muddy shoes.

"Here. Let me get you a newspaper," Helda bustled.

Maggie followed her into the kitchen and obediently set her shoes on the newspaper Helda laid on the floor in a corner. The kitchen was dry and warm, and Maggie gratefully sank into the chair Buff now offered her.

"Will you have a cup of coffee with us?" Helda invited.

"I'd be delighted," Maggie replied, with a sigh. "I'm suddenly very tired." She leaned her elbows on the white-painted table and sighed again. "I feel like it's been a long day. What time is it?"

"Nearly four o'clock," Dr. Friedmann said, pronouncing "o'clock" with German precision. "It has been a long day for all of us. I did not see you at the service this morning."

"No, I was house-sitting next door," Maggie said.

"Ah! And did you find any clues?" Helda asked, setting a steaming cup of coffee in front of Maggie and another in front of Buff.

"Well, I don't—you caught me, didn't you! Yes, I did look around, and no, I didn't find anything very useful. I do think I'll follow up on the group Nora went to in KC that weekend. Maybe something happened there that would give us an idea. Maybe she met someone there, and they followed her home?"

"Perhaps," Buff nodded.

"The family are still convinced it was suicide," Maggie said. "But you didn't think Nora was suicide-prone, right?"

"Why do the family cling to that idea?" Helda asked, sitting down beside Maggie at the table.

"Orin said they didn't see how anyone else could have gotten into the house."

"Perhaps it is easier to think of losing a loved one to suicide than to murder?" Buff suggested. "Or perhaps one of them has something to hide."

"Do you think so? I thought maybe they just wanted it to be over," Maggie said.

"That could be also, but you know as well as I that most murders are committed by members of the family or intimate friends," Buff reminded her.

"So what is your theory, Herr Professor?" Helda teased gently.

"I do not have a theory," he said. "However, I would look for someone whom Nora had hurt deeply, someone who felt she had taken away from them something of value. Unfortunately, that could be any one of many people who knew her." He shook his head sadly.

"The police have questioned Sondra," Maggie began. She did not dare repeat outright what Carl had said, but she desperately wanted Dr. Friedmann's insights. "Surely she couldn't be a suspect."

"The police will have questioned all the neighbors," Buff said. "And all of Nora's friends and family. And, yes, of course Sondra is a suspect. So would you be, if they knew you were so interested." (He pronounced it "in-ter-res-ted.")

"But I'm only interested because—you're teasing me again."

"Indeed. But Sondra must be a suspect. She lives next door, she was once married to a man who became involved with Nora, the families have been entwined for some years. Murders have been committed on far less ground than this."

Maggie shuddered. She would not believe it, she told herself firmly. Besides, on Sunday night, Sondra was—where?

Actually Maggie didn't know. She guessed she needed to talk to Sondra at the first opportunity.

"And do you consider Sondra a likely murderer?" Maggie said, glancing toward the door with sudden apprehension, lest they might be overheard.

"Not likely. Possible. And there are many other 'possibles' among those we know, even among those in this house today," Dr. Friedmann pronounced sententiously.

"Now, Buff, stop it," Helda chided sharply. "Maggie, dear, do not let him bother you. He is being theoretical. He doesn't really think one of our friends is a murderer. Do you, dear?"

"Huh!" was all either of them got out of him.

"Well, I really must be going," Maggie said, after a few moments of silence. "It's been lovely to visit with you both, and thanks for the coffee." She stood up.

"You aren't staying for the Equinox celebration?" Helda asked.

"No, I just came to help with the water, and it seems to be pretty well under control now. Goodbye." She reached down to give Helda a gentle hug. "Goodbye, Herr Doctor Friedmann," she said to Buff.

"Goodbye, Maggie," the two elders said in unison. They all laughed.

"Goodbye," they all three said together, and then chuckled good-naturedly at their own confusion.

Maggie turned and walked quickly through the doorway into the hall, where she almost collided with Leslie Stone. "Whoops! Hello again," she said gaily, still giggling inside.

"I'm about to go, Maggie. Would you like a ride home?" Les said.

"Oh, I don't really need a ride, Les. It's only a block."

"Well, you might as well ride. I'm going now, if you are ready," Les insisted.

"Okay, sure, thanks," Maggie said. "Let me say goodbye to Sondra."

"Do you have to go?" Sondra asked, when Maggie found her putting wet towels in the washer. "I'd be glad if you could stay. We are going ahead with Equinox, and I do need to visit with you."

"No," Maggie said, shaking her head. "I need to get on home." Then, remembering, she added, "But I'd like to talk to you, too. Maybe we could get together this evening."

"After dinner, then? Call me," Sondra said. "Just a minute." She dried her hands on her jeans, and gave Maggie a warm hug. "Thank you so much for being my friend," she said simply.

Maggie returned the hug, feeling a twinge of disloyalty for her earlier conversation with the Friedmanns. "Okay, I'll call you, or you call me when you are ready. See you later, then." She left Sondra, stopping by the kitchen to pick up her shoes, and went outside to find Les waiting for her.

CHAPTER 12

In the front passenger seat of Les's battered VW Bug, Maggie sat leaning forward to avoid being poked in the head by the corner of a large sheet of corrugated cardboard that lay diagonally across the entire back seat.

"Uh, sorry about that box," Les said, when he noticed her discomfort. "Sondra, uh, said she didn't have any, oh, uh, any use for it, and uh, I can use it in a building project."

"It won't be in my way for long," Maggie said, thinking as she hunched over her now-superfluous umbrella and raincoat that she would have much preferred walking to being "cornered" in this way. Why Les hadn't thought of what he was carrying in his car before he offered her a ride? she grumbled to herself.

But rather than dwell on her annoyance, she'd better make the most of the moment. "Les," she said, as he backed out of Sondra's driveway, "can you tell me anything about what happened to Nora at Kathy Gegeshina's house that weekend, anything that might suggest why someone might have wanted to kill Nora?"

"What?" Les seemed startled. "At…in, uh, in Kansas City, you mean? Oh, no, I don't think so! I'm sure there wasn't…I mean, I would have noticed if….No, no, I'm quite sure not. No, nothing."

"I'm sorry to have to probe, since I know you and Nora were friends," Maggie said. "But could you just tell me a little of what did go on at your weekends? Just to give me an idea what they were like?"

"I, uh, it's hard to describe," Les said. He paused, as though in deep thought as he drove into Maggie's driveway and switched off the ignition. Then he turned a bit sideways toward Maggie, leaning one arm on the back of the bucket seat. "Baba is, as I said, uh, as I said earlier, is, oh, a fully enlightened being," he began.

"Yes, but what does that mean in terms of your group?" Maggie queried.

"Uh, that means he is fully, expressing, yes, uh, the Godhead in himself, just by being who he, uh, truly is. He is able to assist, that is, assist others just by, yes, by being who he is, by his presence, without doing anything, uh, anything in particular." Les seemed to be warming to his subject, as his speech gradually became slightly more fluent. "Baba's energy is such that, when one is touched by him, uh, one understands or sees, yes, sees in a way not possible before, and yet, one also wants more and more insight."

Hoping to get Les to focus more about the group members, Maggie started to interject a question. But he seemed not to notice.

"Oh, uh," he continued, now gazing not directly at Maggie but past her, toward the redbud tree at the corner of the house next door. "Baba is working with me on my, uh, diet, you know, and on other things. He, uh, sometimes teaches by paradox, or, uh, by joking and story-telling. Oh, yes, and he, well, he loves to tell stories. I, uh, once heard him tell, uh, the story of the cobra who, uh, well, he was biting people, you know, and he was, well, the Master told him, yes, told him to stop biting people."

I had to ask, didn't I, Maggie castigated herself.

"So, the cobra did, did stop, that is," Les continued, "and when the village children learned, you know, learned he wouldn't bite, well, they began mistreating the cobra unmercifully. Yes, unmercifully. So, uh, the snake complained to the, uh, yes, to the Master." Les's face was fixed in a rhapsodic smile, apparently attendant on the recollection of Baba's teaching.

So the snake complained to the Master, Maggie thought,

her hand on the car door handle. Yes, Les, get it over with—and the Master said…

"So the Master, uh, oh, the Master said to the cobra, 'Oh, uh, I, uh….'" Les continued, clearly oblivious to Maggie's growing impatience.

'I never said you couldn't hiss!' Maggie thought, and bit her tongue to keep from reciting the punchline of the old tale ahead of Les.

"And the Master said, 'I never told you, you know, not to hiss!'"

"Yes, that's a great story," Maggie said quickly, getting out of the car. "Well, thanks, Les, thanks a lot."

"You know…" Les leaned across the car so that the corner of the cardboard almost jabbed him in the Adam's apple. Maggie paused, her hand still on the door. "You know, you really shouldn't be poking around in this, Nora's murder. Leave, uh, the detecting to the police. They'll work things out, and it's, uh, much safer that way."

You sound like Mike, Maggie thought. But she said only, "Thanks. Thanks again for the ride, Les," as she fished in her bag for her house keys.

Walking toward the front door, she continued feeling around inside the roomy bag. Suddenly she had a vision of herself dropping keys and everything else inside the door as she ran for the phone a few hours earlier. "Oh, sh-hakespeare!" she muttered, giving the bag a hard shake that confirmed (by the absence of jangle) that her keys were indeed still lying on the floor on the other side of the locked door.

Returning to the front corner of the house, she dug under the plastic for the spare key. This was getting to be a habit! As she walked back toward the door, she noticed that Les was still sitting in the driveway. Such a gentleman. She waved the key at him, hoping he would take that as a sign he didn't need to wait to see her safely inside. But he continued to sit there watching until she had unlocked the door and opened it.

As Maggie put the key back into its hiding place, Les finally put the car into gear and backed down the driveway. "Bye-bye," she mouthed, and waved. What a strange man, she thought, as he waved back. And maybe the last person to see Nora alive. She shivered—except for the murderer, of course.

Inside, Maggie's first act was to pick up her errant keys from the floor and drop them ceremoniously into her bag, before slinging the bag and contents onto a step above the landing. Mike kept telling her it was bad policy to leave a handbag near the front door—an invitation to casual thievery—but it was so convenient!

Checking the clock, she decided she had time for a hot shower before she needed to start supper. Upstairs, she paused outside her son's bedroom. "Hello?" she called, giving the closed door a couple of taps. "You there, Geoff?"

Taking a muffled sound from within as permission to enter, she opened the door and took a step into the room, one step being about as far as she could have walked without stepping on or tripping over the potpourri of socks, cassette tapes, sweats, school newspapers, and other assorted paraphernalia common to the habitat of the teenaged American male (suburban).

"Hi, Mom, how's it goin'?" Geoff grinned up at her from his bed, where he sat with radio-cassette player close at hand and a textbook open on his outstretched legs.

"Oh, fine. And with you?" Maggie smiled fondly at her only son, a slimmer, curly-haired version of Mike, with the same high cheekbones and quiet dark eyes.

"Not bad. *Beaucoup* homework tonight, though. Got a test in History tomorrow, and a scene for Players. When's dinner?"

"About six, as usual, if that suits you and Mike," Maggie said, trying to remember whether Mike had said anything about working late.

"Sure. Just give me a call, Mom," said Geoff, turning his music up a notch and settling back to his book.

Thus dismissed, Maggie went to take her shower. Half an

hour later, her towel-dried hair in damp ringlets, she was in the kitchen stirring a skillet of browning hamburger and chopped onions when she heard a knock at the front door. Pausing to turn down the heat under the sizzling meat, she went to the door, to find Kara Patterson waiting outside.

"Why, Kara! Come in," Maggie said, surprised.

"Thank you, Mrs. Tenwhistle. I'm—do you have time? You said I could come by if I needed to talk. And I guess I do."

"Of course. Come on in," Maggie invited, wondering if this had anything to do with the scene in Sondra's bedroom earlier in the afternoon. She led the way down into the living room and motioned to the couch, taking a seat herself.

Kara sat down on the edge of the couch, her back stiff, hands on her knees. Her designer jeans and stylish canvas shoes showed signs of earlier soaking. Even with her shoulders hunched forward, her Smiley-Face t-shirt was just tight enough revealed the curve of the small, firm breasts beneath. She was a lovely young woman, just a year older than Alyssa if Maggie remembered correctly. If this Jas fellow wasn't her boyfriend, she undoubtedly had one somewhere around.

As if in answer to Maggie's unspoken question, Kara suddenly burst out, "Did you hear the song he sang—no, of course you didn't. You weren't there. Well, he came up and sang at the memorial service, and it was like a love song—for my mother! It was disgusting!" She grimaced and repeated, almost shouting, "It was disgusting!"

"Mmmm." Maggie searched for something comforting or otherwise appropriate to say. "I can imagine how you feel" didn't seem quite right, since she didn't have a clue. "Who was this?" she finally asked. If she couldn't be helpful, she might as well satisfy her own intense curiosity.

"Harrison Creitz," Kara said, not seeming to notice Maggie's discombobulation. "He's a student at Washburn. He and I are...well, we have been...we were dating. Oh, I don't know. I can't..." She covered her face with one hand and drew a long quivering breath.

Abruptly, Kara stood up and walked to the window. "I loved my mother, Mrs. Tenwhistle, in spite of what she was, but I can't seem to feel sorry she's gone. She was not a very nice person."

"Perhaps you're still under a lot of stress, Kara. You may see it differently after the passage of time. Time does heal…" Maggie knew she was sounding trite. "Would you like to talk about it?" she asked, changing her tone.

"I knew my mother had lots of men," Kara said. "She had them before my father left and she had them after he left. And when she got into all this Tantric guru stuff, they were around her like flies. She flaunted them in front of us all. But I never thought she'd try to take my boyfriend away from me!"

"Your mother was seeing this Harrison Creitz?" Maggie tried to keep her incredulity out of her voice.

"We had a fight—early on the Friday evening before she… died. I went over to have it out with her. She said it was a matter of freedom of choice, that I was being naive and old-fashioned. 'It's what we fought for back in the Sixties,' she said. 'It's part of the new paradigm. People can't possess people anymore.' It felt like, like she was taunting me. Oh, Mrs. Tenwhistle! I just don't believe it!"

Kara's voice rose to a wail and she swung around to face Maggie, who had come up to stand beside her at the window. Maggie held out her arms and the young woman took a half step forward, allowing herself to be enfolded. She put her head on Maggie's shoulder, her body shaking with silent sobs.

Long, damp moments later, Kara raised her head. Maggie released her and went to get a tissue box, pausing to turn off the stove under the thoroughly cooked hamburger. If Mike and Geoff had to wait for supper, they'd just have to wait!

"Kara," Maggie said cautiously, after Kara had blown her nose, "Kara, you said you and your mother fought. Are you trying to tell me that you…?"

Kara stared at Maggie, open-mouthed. "Oh, no, Mrs.

Tenwhistle! No! No, my mother and I yelled at each other, and I slammed the door on the way out, but she was very much alive when I left late Friday afternoon, and I didn't see her again."

Maggie nodded gravely.

"That's what's so damn...frustrating!" Kara continued, her voice rising in volume as she spoke. "I hate what she did, and what she's still doing, to me, to my father, my sister, to Lorraine. Even though she's dead, she's still messing up our lives. I hate it! Maybe I even hate her. But I didn't kill her!"

Maggie nodded again, listening attentively

"Anyway, she died on Sunday, not Friday night," Kara said, her voice dropping as though she was running out of energy. "Dad and Lorraine and I spent all day Saturday at the Nelson, and Saturday night we went to the Civic Theater, and I stayed overnight with them, and then Sunday I was with friends all day—so I didn't even see her again." This last was very soft, and Kara's lips quivered as she finished speaking.

Afraid Kara was about to burst into tears again, Maggie said quickly, "I wasn't accusing you, Kara. Please believe me. I just wanted to understand what you were saying." Maggie paused, then went on in a different tone, "Would you like a drink of water or a cup of tea?"

"Oh, no, thanks. I guess I'd better be going. Actually, I feel better, having talked with someone," Kara said. "Thank you, Mrs. Tenwhistle." She moved toward the door.

"Please feel free to come by any time," Maggie said, walking with her up the steps and opening the door. "I'm always glad to listen."

As Maggie returned to her dinner preparations, she considered what she had learned. Not much, really. Mostly just enough to raise a lot more questions. Was Harrison Creitz the blondish young man with the Oriental vase? If so, what was he doing at Sondra's? Who was Jas? Had Nora really seduced her daughter's boyfriend? How much ill will did Orin still harbor toward his ex? If, as Kara said, Nora had "flaunted" her affairs before as well as after her divorce, might even the most open-minded husband have felt a level of humiliation that could still rankle?

After turning up the heat under the skillet, Maggie poured the contents of two cans of tomatoes over the hamburger and added a cup of long-grain brown rice. It wasn't hard to imagine that Orin, or his daughter, or even his second wife, might feel Nora had, in Buff Friedmann's phrase, "taken away from them something of value." Of course, that was clearly true for Sondra also. Maggie stirred the Spanish rice thoughtfully. The picture of Nora that was emerging was of a much more complex and fascinating person than Maggie would have guessed from their brief meeting.

Was Kara Patterson subtle enough—and a good enough actress—for the whole scene to have been a performance? Designed to create the illusion of an ingenuous, and therefore innocent, confession of both motive and opportunity? If so, why had Maggie been the audience, rather than the police?

And what was Les Stone's relationship with the dead woman? He hadn't given Maggie any real information about the other members of the Kansas City group, which was disappointing, since what had happened there seemed the best bet for getting a handle on someone from "outside" who might have had cause to want Nora dead.

Maggie put a lid on the skillet and began fixing a salad.

If Nora was "seeing" a man young enough to be her son, had she really learned Tantric secrets that made her irresistible? Or was he some kind of gold-digger? It seemed unlikely that Nora had a fortune, but one never knew.

The possibility of finding answers to most of her questions seemed to Maggie to be remote. But she could make inquiries about some of them, she realized, and she could try to contact that Kathy Gegeshina in Kansas City, to find out if she'd noticed anything strange about Nora. I'll call her tonight, Maggie resolved, as she finished setting the table.

"Hello, honey," she called out to her husband, who had just come in. "Supper's ready. You can call Geoff if you want to, and we can eat. Unless you want to hang out for a little first."

"No, I'd just as soon eat," Mike said, coming into the kitchen and giving Maggie a light kiss on the lips. "It's been a long day!"

"More problems with the coroner statistics project?" Maggie knew Mike had had to report the Clerks' polite but emphatic refusal to be tempted by visions of new staff.

"Yes, and some personnel problems, and a complaint on an agent, but I don't really want to think about it any more. Geoff's in his room?"

"Studying, last I knew. Bless the boy, he really is a good lad!" Maggie said.

"He'll do," Mike smiled, going to the stairs to call his son to dinner.

"Want to help me with the dishes, Geoff?" Mike said after they had finished their meal.

"Well, Dad, I really have a lot of homework," Geoff began.

"Just leave them, Mike," Maggie urged. "We can get them later."

"You spoil him," Mike cautioned, as Geoff made his escape. "How's he going to learn to be a liberated man if he never has to clean up?"

"How did you learn it?" Maggie teased. "Certainly not from your mother!"

"Nope! From my wife! And it was a painful lesson. I want to spare Geoff that hardship." He smiled, and held out his arms to Maggie, who warmly returned his embrace, laying her head on her husband's broad chest.

"I need to go down and see Sondra for a little while tonight. You won't feel lonesome?"

"I'll just watch some tv and veg out," Mike replied, still holding her. "You won't be late, will you? I know you'll be careful."

"No, I won't be very late," Maggie said, lifting her head to look up into Mike's bronze face, unlined except for just a few crinkles at the corners of his eyes. "In fact, I need to call her now to be sure if it's going to work at all."

CHAPTER 13

As it turned out, Sondra was occupied with her guests and her potluck when Maggie phoned. She promised to call back just as soon as she was free. Maggie did the dishes by herself, then read the morning paper, and spent a frustrating hour trying to concentrate on some investment articles she had laid aside weeks ago. "I thought you were going to Sondra's," Mike remarked, looking up from his book at around 9:45.

"I am, if she ever calls," Maggie said. "I should have known better than to expect her to be ready at a reasonable time."

Just then the phone rang. It was Sondra, all sweetness and apologies, and hoping so very much that Maggie could still come down. Of course, Maggie could.

On the way to Sondra's house, she reminded herself of the things she needed to find out. First, did Sondra have an alibi for Sunday night, and if so, was it solid? What had she told the police that made them consider her a prime suspect?

Who was Harrison Creitz, and did Sondra know anything about his relationship to Nora? It seemed likely she would, since she knew Harrison and lived next door to Nora. Who was Jas, and how did he fit into the picture? And what more, if anything, could Sondra tell Maggie about the mysterious Kansas City group and its guru?

When Maggie arrived, Sondra greeted her warmly. "Will you have some tea? The water's already hot," she offered after Maggie was comfortably seated in a corner of the worn plush-cushioned couch in the living room.

"If it's not too much trouble, yes, thanks," Maggie said.

"Sleepytime?" Sondra called from the kitchen.

Not quite, but getting very close, Maggie thought. "Fine, thanks," she called out.

Back with two mugs of the soothing tea, Sondra handed one to Maggie and settled herself in the other corner of the couch, her chartreuse-stockinged feet tucked under her. "So, how are you?" she asked Maggie.

"Oh, I'm fine, just tired. And you? Everything okay? Nothing ruined by the flood?"

"Actually, hardly any damage at all. You can see that the rug is still damp along the edge. As it turned out, it was hardly worth taking it outside. We brought it back in before people left so it wouldn't get 'dewed' on."

"Mmhm," Maggie nodded. "So most of your helpers were here for the Equinox celebration?"

"All but Orin and Kara and you," Sondra said. "They came over because I called and asked them for help. They were still at Nora's house, and I didn't think they'd mind. They left soon after you did."

"Who were the young men? I don't think I've seen them before," Maggie ventured.

"Well, you know I've been working with the oral history project at the high school? Harrison Creitz was a student I met in that work a year or two ago, and he was interested in Native American spirituality and earth religions and such, so he's been coming to some of these seasonal celebrations. He's quite a gifted musician, a really talented person."

"Do you know if he knew Nora?"

"I think he did, actually. They may have been at a few events at the same time. Why do you ask?" Sondra said, brushing a strand of blond hair away from her face.

"Kara came down to my place—after she left here, I suppose," Maggie said, "and she told me the most astonishing tale. She said that she and Harrison—he's the young man with the beard, right? Who, I heard, sang at the memorial service this morning?" Sondra nodded. "That she and Harrison had been dating, and that recently he had been 'seeing' Nora instead! Could that possibly be right? Does it make any sense to you?" Maggie paused. Sondra didn't reply. "Kara seemed terribly upset about the whole thing," Maggie continued, "and if it's true, I can't say I much blame her."

Sondra sighed. "They say you should never speak ill of the dead, Maggie," she said. "Actually, I try never to speak ill of anyone, so I'd be breaking my own rule, not someone else's." She looked at Maggie. "I'm sure you've heard about our past history, Nora and me?"

Maggie nodded. "Just a little, not much really. I guess it was before you and I knew each other."

"No point in hashing it all over," Sondra said. She seemed to come to a decision. "Suffice it to say, I know from personal experience that Nora Patterson is not one to be deterred from taking what she wants just because someone else thinks it belongs to them." She clenched her jaw and breathed another long sigh.

Maggie waited.

"Maybe it never would have worked out between Sam and me," Sondra continued, looking fixedly at her left foot. "There's no way of knowing. Forgiveness is something one works on day by day. I believe in forgiveness. I think if you want to live in a world where there is forgiveness, you have to have it go both ways. That's what it means."

Maggie nodded understanding. "Hmmmm."

"She had done it before, and she's done it many times since. I don't see why anyone would be surprised, least of all Kara," Sondra said after a silence.

"What surprised me the most was the age differential. I mean, he's Kara's age, surely, not that much older than Geoff. He's got to be more than twenty years Nora's junior," Maggie said, shaking her head. "Somehow, I can't—"

"I guess I don't really feel comfortable talking about this," Sondra interrupted. "Can we change the subject?

"Sure," Maggie said. "I've been wanting to ask you what more you can tell me about this Kansas City group that Nora was going to. Did you ever go? Do you know what they did up there?"

"No, I never went," Sondra said, shaking her head in a decisive gesture that seemed almost to turn into a shudder. "I really don't know much more about it than what Kara told us Monday night. Nora did invite me. It was clear she thought the sessions were very worthwhile. I think the emphasis was on clearing away blocks—blocks to more, I don't know, enlightened living or something. Sounded good, but a little more adventurous than I really want, I guess."

"What do you mean, more adventurous? Did they do drugs, or yoga, or have orgies, or what?" Maggie asked.

"Nothing that strenuous, that I know of," Sondra smiled. "No, just, it seemed like Baba Sindy, or whatever his name was, asked for a lot—his approach was very stringent, and whatever you did you had to do it all the way. Like Nora's giving up eating everything but nuts and fruit juices. It seemed rather extreme to me, is all. But maybe that was just Nora. I don't know."

"How long had she been going to these sessions? Do you know? Each one was over a weekend?"

"I don't really know, Maggie. Why are you so interested?" Sondra frowned and looked down at her hands.

"Sorry, just curious, I guess," Maggie said. "Can I ask just one more quick question? How long did she usually stay? Do you know when she left and when she came back that last weekend?"

"I think she usually went up on Friday evening and came back some time late Sunday afternoon. Actually, I think I saw Les come to pick her up last Friday evening—but I don't remember seeing her come home." Sondra yawned, making no effort to cover her indifference to this topic of discussion.

"Sorry," Maggie said quickly. "You said you needed to talk to me. What is that about?"

"I needed to have you think through with me why the police want me to come down tomorrow for more 'discussion.'

I've already told them everything I know about the day Nora was killed, which isn't much. It rained all day. I was here, but I didn't see any comings and goings over there, because I wasn't looking. I was reading a book, and I just sat and read all day, since it was too wet to go anywhere. I got up to check the patio occasionally, but that's all."

"Did you go out in the evening?" Maggie asked.

"No, because I got engrossed in the book, and I just kept on reading. I went to bed about 11:00, I guess, because that's when I finished the book. I don't know what more I can tell them." Sondra managed to sound defensive and plaintive at the same time.

"Sondra," Maggie said, looking directly at her friend, "why do you think they want to talk to you again?"

"I suppose they are desperate for clues and are hoping I've noticed or thought of something else, but I haven't," Sondra said, her gray eyes shadowed.

"Do you think they might consider you a suspect?" Maggie felt reluctant to say outright what she knew.

"Oh, I suppose that's possible," Sondra said airily, "but they surely have better candidates." She seemed to dismiss the idea.

Maggie wasn't ready to let it go. "But you don't have a confirmed alibi? Nobody can vouch for where you were Sunday night?"

"No, I was here alone."

"And you have a key to Nora's place?"

"Had. I gave it back to Karin when we went over with the food. But anybody who knew Nora could have gotten in if Nora let them in. Right?" Sondra seemed a bit more concerned now.

"Anybody could have gotten in, but who could have gotten out? The doors and windows were all locked, except the door between the kitchen and the garage. All the doors have dead bolts that work with a key. And the garage door only works with the electronic twanger in the car, because the button inside is disconnected or something."

Maggie looked at Sondra, who was staring across the room at the Oriental vase, now restored to its rightful place on top of a polished walnut pedestal. The elegant, luxurious effect seemed out of place in Sondra's otherwise rather dowdy decor.

"Did you know Nora kept a gun in her house, Sondra?" Maggie pursued.

"What are you? Rehearsing me for the police?" Sondra snapped. "That's what they asked me the first time."

"Well, it's a legitimate question," Maggie said. "Look, Sondra, I'm your friend. I'm trying to help you."

"I know, Maggie. I'm sorry, I guess I do know that I could be considered a suspect, and I'm trying not to know it." Sondra stood and began to pace back and forth across the room. "It seems so unfair, because there have been months at a stretch in the past several years when I would have gladly killed that woman, when I felt I would be doing the world a favor, and now when I've finally pretty much gotten over it and don't get a stomachache every time I see her, somebody else does it. And I'm getting all this hassle." She sank back onto the couch and took a long deep breath, letting it out all at once through her nose so it made a sound like an animal snorting.

Maggie wanted to comfort her friend, but she also wanted to help her, and she wasn't sure the two aims were compatible. "Sondra, I want to find out who really did kill Nora." she said. "If the police think you did it, they may not be looking very hard for anyone else. So we have to help them. Okay?"

Sondra nodded, looking drawn and tired, as though her last speech had exhausted her.

"So can you stick with me long enough to answer one or two more questions?" Sondra nodded again, without enthusiasm.

"So did you know where Nora's gun was? And who else would have known?" Maggie asked, trying to make the questions sound as casual as possible.

"Actually, I did know where it was, at one time, anyway.

She used to keep it in a drawer in the little table in the front hall. I saw it there once when I was looking for a pencil." Sondra frowned.

"Well, if the police didn't ask you that before, they are pretty sure to this time," Maggie speculated. "Did it strike you as strange that a pacifist would keep a handgun?"

"Not at the time—it was years ago, before, when we first knew them. But it does seem strange now that I think about it," Sondra replied thoughtfully. "I wonder—oh, well, what does it matter now?"

"Just that we're trying to understand Nora so we can figure out who might have killed her. Who else that you know of had a key to her house?" Maggie felt she was finally getting some useful answers.

"I guess the two girls. I don't know who else. Maybe Harrison, if what Kara says is true," Sondra responded, looking more interested also.

"Orin?"

"I wouldn't think so. I certainly never saw him come over here. I don't think he and Nora were on that kind of terms, at least not since he remarried."

"How long has he been remarried?" Maggie asked.

"A year, maybe a little longer, I think. I don't really know him, but judging from Nora's attitude, I think it's not been too very long. His new wife is somebody I'd never heard of."

"Oh?" Maggie raised her eyebrows. "What was Nora's attitude?"

"I had the impression she was jealous," Sondra said, smiling slightly. "It seemed ironic, but I had the feeling she was more than a little annoyed that Orin had found someone else after all these years!"

"And speaking of new people," Maggie said, aware she was stretching a point but determined to get one last question in, "who was that dark-haired young man who was helping with the carpet yesterday? Did he come over with Kara and Orin, or is he somebody you know?"

Sondra looked sharply at Maggie and then sank back against the cushions again. "Oh, he's a friend, a friend of Harrison's," she said wearily. "You know, I think I really have to get to bed, Maggie," she concluded, yawning.

"Yeah, it's time for me to go," Maggie agreed.

"Thanks for coming down," Sondra said, leading the way to the door. "And thanks for helping this afternoon. I'm sorry you couldn't stay for the ritual. We had colored eggs and dandelion greens and the whole works."

"Glad to help, and I'm glad nothing was really hurt by the water," Maggie said. "I hope everything goes well tomorrow. I'm sure it will," she added as she saw an anxious look come over Sondra's features. "Don't worry about it," she soothed. "You know you didn't do it, so ultimately you have nothing to worry about. Right?"

"Right! Well, goodnight. And thanks again."

The two women exchanged a quick goodby hug, and Maggie left, deliberate steps taking her down the dark street toward her own house, as she pondered what she'd learned.

When she arrived at home, she found Mike had already gone to bed, where he was reading a paperback novel. Maggie quickly got undressed and began her brief evening toilet. As she rinsed her face and brushed her teeth, she thought about Sondra and the way her attitude had seemed to move from almost flip to anxious to apathetic. She was not going to be much help in helping herself, if indeed she needed help. Which she almost assuredly did.

Maggie agreed with Nora's family, she decided, in preferring that the death have been a suicide. Nora was a woman nobody much liked and for unknown personal reasons she decided to take her own life. That was not especially pleasant, but at least it was tidy. This murder business was messy and painful for those left behind, especially since it looked nearly certain the killer was someone well-known to Nora. Someone like Kara, or Orin, or Sondra.

Maggie had been close enough to numerous law enforcement investigations over the years to know that detectives were only human and were eager for quick closure. The messiness of an unsolved case was uncomfortable to them, and they were likely not to be very active in pursuing alternatives if they thought they had zeroed in on the perpetrator. If they had pegged Sondra, their energies now would be mostly devoted to making the case. This was a hazard Mike had always emphasized with his detectives, but he was as susceptible as anyone else. It was just human nature, once you thought you'd solve the puzzle, to work on how the last few pieces fit. Nobody wanted to think about tearing it all up and starting over with a different face.

So, Maggie concluded, it was up to her to try to find something, anything, to upset their complacency. A significant fact of some kind that didn't fit their picture. Heading back to the bedroom, she stopped at the foot of the bed. It was nearly 11:00, but her mind was whirling. "Mike," she said, "I think I'm going to go back downstairs for a little bit before I go to bed."

"Sure, Tiger," Mike said, glancing up from his book. "You okay?"

"I'm fine," Maggie said. "I'm concerned about Sondra, though. You haven't heard any more from Carl, have you?"

"What? No, I haven't. But I wouldn't have expected to." His eyes returned to his book.

"Maybe you could call him again sometime soon and see what else you can find out. Would you do that for me, Mike?" Maggie knew she was taking unfair advantage, that he was more than likely to agree just in order to get her to stop talking.

"Okay," he murmured, not looking up.

Maggie put on a robe and went downstairs. She got her tarot deck from the shelf and took it to the sofa, where she settled herself back against the arm, legs tucked under her. She opened the wooden box and unwrapped the cards, spreading the blue scarf on the couch in front of her.

The question? She pondered, and after discarding several

other formulations, settled on "What do I need to know about this situation in order to help Sondra?"

Moving slowly but purposefully, she shuffled the cards several times. She divided the thoroughly-shuffled deck into three piles, and reassembled the piles with the center stack on top. Then, working more briskly, she dealt out eleven cards. The first card turned up, which she placed just left of center on the scarf, showed what Maggie thought of as "the Ice Queen," an imperial-looking woman in white fur robes, standing on a snowy hillock, her hand outstretched to a large white bird soaring above her. "'Queen of Swords,' what it's all about," Maggie said, half-aloud.

"Helps me, crosses me, coming from, going toward, at the root of it, highest possible outcome"—reciting the designations under her breath, she rapidly placed the rest of the cards in their appointed spots in the traditional Celtic spread. Then she set aside the remainder of the deck and gazed meditatively at the cards before her.

The first card Maggie focused on was the Son of Swords, an arrogant-looking man with a dagger in one hand and a dead bird in the other. Yes, Maggie thought, I already knew we were dealing with a murder. You didn't have to tell me that.

At least, however, this card in the place in the spread representing the root of the matter reassured her that the layout was a response to the question she had asked—it was about murder! Cruel or at least selfish behavior, or merely impulsive behavior, as the man glanced from the treasure at his feet to another treasure trove a few yards away, as though unable to decide which to grab next.

Maggie picked up one of the central cards, the Four of Discs, with a picture of the interior of a small house, and a woman shutting the door, as if shutting out the world. Helps to keep to myself? she wondered. Yes, that made sense with the challenge card, which featured a circle of friends all engaged in helping a birthing mother. Perhaps this was suggesting that not all in the circle were really friends. Sharing her most intimate thoughts, even with those who seemed to want to help, could be a hindrance rather than a help, at this stage. Better to "close the door" and keep her own counsel for the time being.

The "inner environment" card was the Empress, goddess of love, lounging on her couch in the garden. Nora? As she was, or as she saw herself? "Hopes and fears" were represented by the Moon—a mysterious card that seemed to Maggie to portend a nightmarish world, in which nothing was quite what it seemed to be. And the most probable outcome, signified by the card at the top of the spread, was the Wheel of Fortune.

"And when you're up, you're up, And when you're down, you're down, And when you're only half-way up, you're neither up nor down," Maggie sang softly, sweeping the cards together and wrapping them in the silk scarf once more. The Grand Old Duke of York had nothing on her, she decided. Right now, she was down, and she knew it. If she was to find the answer to this riddle, she'd better hope to catch the upward turn of the wheel. What she needed was a clue, any clue. She put the cards back into the box and went to bed, suddenly feeling worn out from a day that had, after all, been much fuller than she could possibly have anticipated.

CHAPTER 14

The next morning, Maggie woke early from a dream that fled completely but left her with an uneasy feeling. Her thoughts went immediately to the murder and her unsatisfactory conversation with Sondra. She rolled over and tried to go back to sleep, but it was no use. When she heard Geoff moving around in the kitchen, she got up quietly without disturbing Mike, threw on a cotton robe, and descended the stairs. "Morning, Geoff," she said softly. "Mind if I join you?"

"Hi, Mom." He looked up from his breakfast. "Sure, have a chair."

Maggie started a cup of tea and leaned against the counter, looking fondly at her son. "Geoff," she said on a sudden impulse, "do you know a guy named Jas, who might have gone to West, or another fellow named Harrison Creitz—maybe about a year or two ahead of Alyssa, I'd say. Know anything about either of them?"

"Jason Wickers? And what was the other guy's name? Creitz? I think I might know who he is. Jason Wickers was a big football star, graduated two, no, three years ago. I was still in middle school."

"And Harrison Creitz?"

"He might have been in Alyssa's class, or a year ahead. Does he have kind of reddish hair?"

Maggie nodded.

"Yeah, he had the lead in *Carousel*. A real party dude. That bunch were fairly heavy into drugs." Mike walked into the kitchen as Geoff finished his last gulp of orange juice. "That's according to legend, of course, Mom," he added hastily. "You could ask Alyssa; it would have been the class just ahead of her."

"Did you know Kara Patterson? She was in *Midsummer* with Alyssa." Maggie looked at Geoff, willing him to stay just a little longer before rushing off to his zero-hour class.

"Can't say I really knew her. Know who she is. She's at Washburn, I think. Oh—is her mother the dead-ee? Sorry, Mom," he said, as he caught his father's scowl. "The deceased. I hadn't thought about that connection."

"I hadn't either until I saw Kara at her mother's house," Maggie said. "Should I have told Alyssa? It didn't even occur to me to say anything."

"I don't know, Mom. Why?" He stood and moved toward the door.

"Well, I mean, would she want to send a card or something?"

"I don't know about that. I don't think they were really friends particularly. Just fellow thespians." And with that, Geoff made his escape upstairs.

"What was that about the heavy drug scene?" Mike asked Maggie, as he leaned against the counter, sipping his coffee.

"I was asking about some kids I met at Sondra's yesterday. They seem to be friends of Sondra's, and one of them used to date Kara Patterson. And Kara says her mother had bewitched him, before she died."

"Friends of Sondra? But they're Alyssa's age?" Mike looked puzzled.

"Sondra has friends of all ages, from eighty to eight. She collects fascinating and odd specimens. Come to think of it, that's one of the reasons I continue to be intrigued with her. If she were only challenging, I could probably avoid her. But she has all these neat and strange people who seem to value her, and I guess that makes her more interesting to me."

"And Nora? What did she have to do with these kids?" Mike asked.

"According to Kara—and some other ambiguous evidence—Nora was more than just friends with this Harrison Creitz. Kara had a big blow-up with her mother over it, just before Nora was killed." Maggie got up from the table and carried her empty cup to the sink. "It lends a lurid air to the situation, don't you think?" she said with a wry smile.

"What about the drugs?" Mike said. "We've been so sure about our two. You don't think…"

"No, I don't, not for a minute," Maggie said softly.

"Mom," Geoff's voice came from the stairway. "I'll be late getting home tonight. Don't wait dinner for me. I've promised to help paint sets for *Music Man*."

"When should we expect you, son?" Maggie asked.

"I don't know. Could be late," Geoff called back. He opened the front door. "So long, guys."

"Hey! Wait!" Maggie heard the door bang shut on her words. "*Your* child!" she accused Mike, as she rose to go get dressed.

"Are we going to have lunch together today?" Mike asked.

"What? Oh, I suppose so, yes," Maggie said collecting her thoughts with difficulty. "I don't know of any reason why not."

"You don't seem too enthused about it," Mike said, reaching to wrap an arm around Maggie's waist.

"I'm…that is, I didn't mean to be unfriendly," Maggie said. "I was just thinking about those young people from yesterday, and wonder whether I should try to talk to them."

Going , she seemed anti-climactic after the past twenty-four hours, but Maggie couldn't think of a good reason not to go, so she went. The morning's work proved strictly routine, which was fortunate, since her attention kept wandering to possible implications of the information she'd gleaned from Geoff.

She breathed a prayer of thanks, not for the first time, that she really did not worry about either her son or his sister in relation to abuse of drugs, legal or illegal. Neither of them smoked or drank, so far as she and Mike could determine, and they seemed quite frank about which of their peers did and did not.

As for illegal drugs, she thought neither Alyssa nor Geoff was willing to jeopardize their own futures, or their father's career, by getting into this sphere—although both were more tolerant of the illegal forays of others than Mike and Maggie would have preferred. "But it's a different world they have to live in," Maggie had often said to Mike. "And it's our generation that kicked over many of the barriers that used to make it all lots safer—or at least lots simpler."

So what about these kids she had met recently, she wondered. If Nora Patterson had had anything to do with supplying them—well, then she deserved exactly what she got, if not worse. But somehow that didn't go with anything else Maggie knew about Nora. Most likely just a red herring. An awful lot of those music and theater kids might be experimenting with alcohol and other drugs, but most of the ones she knew, or knew of, seemed to manage to avoid real trouble. Still, there could be a drug connection somehow. Something going on at Washburn? Several people were acting very strangely. Maybe she should try to talk to some of these young folks.

The phone rang, startling Maggie out of her revery. After taking a message for Nelson, who was away for the day, Maggie rummaged in her purse for the notes she had snatched from Nora's message board. Les…Harrison…Kathy, with a Kansas City number…and Pat. Well, she knew now who Les, Kathy, and Harrison probably were. That left "Pat," with a west-central Topeka number that could be in the Washburn area. Maybe a student? Male or female, she couldn't tell.

Maggie glanced at the clock. Nearly 1:00. Mike had called around 10:30 to cancel lunch, and Maggie had just grabbed a bite from the vending machines downstairs. So she'd already worked through her lunch hour.

Terrence would be gone all afternoon. Maggie stood up and walked into Constance's office. "Would it cause any problems if I took off early this afternoon?" she asked. "I have some personal errands to run."

"No problem," Constance said. "I'm going to be here working. Take the whole afternoon if you like. And have a good weekend."

"Thanks. You, too." Maggie returned to her desk, and taking a deep breath, picked up the phone and dialed the number next to the word "Pat" on Nora's message note.

A female voice, probably young, answered after two rings. "Hello?"

"Pat?"

"Yes."

"My name is Maggie Tenwhistle. I'm a neighbor of Nora Patterson, and I, uh, know you were a friend of hers." Suddenly Maggie realized she hadn't thought out what she was going to say. "I don't know whether you...that is, I'm...well, my daughter Alyssa was a schoolmate of Nora's daughter Kara. They were in Players together, and—were you by any chance at West about that same time?" she improvised quickly.

"No, I was at High, but I know Kara." Maggie noted with relief that the voice on the other end of the line sounded mildly interested. "What did you say your daughter's name was?"

"Alyssa Tenwhistle, but she was a year or two behind Kara. She's away at college, Alyssa, that is. Are you at Washburn?"

"Yes?" The answer sounded more like a question, and Maggie knew she had to think of something else quickly.

"Would you have a few minutes to visit with me if I came up to campus this afternoon? I can't reach Kara, and I'd like to talk to someone who knows her before I call Alyssa this evening." Maggie ended in a rush, crossing her fingers for luck. (She should have crossed them for the lie, too, she thought as she waited for Pat's response.)

"Well, I guess so. I'm going up to the library in a few minutes, and we could talk there for just a little bit, if you like."

Maggie imagined the young woman wondering what kind

of a weird stranger she was. "Why, that would be great!" she said. "What time, and where shall I look for you?"

"Could you meet me in about fifteen minutes, just inside the front door? We can find a corner somewhere."

"Okay. I'm short and dark-haired, with a dark blue dress," Maggie said. "Thanks very much. I'll see you in fifteen minutes, then." Hanging up, Maggie made a face. What did she think she was going to learn? She'd probably just made a fool of herself.

Pat turned out to be a bespectacled young woman with wavy dark hair and a face that could have been called "handsome" except for a heavy sprinkling of acne scars. She and Maggie retired to a corner of the Ethel Stone Stauffer Memorial Browsing Area. Seating herself on a sturdy institutional-style sofa with green-gray upholstery, Pat twisted sideways on the ample seat and looked at Maggie expectantly.

"Well," Maggie began in a library sort of half-whisper, "I haven't been able to reach Kara, as I said, and I want to be able to tell Alyssa how she's doing. Have you seen her since yesterday afternoon?"

"No," Pat said levelly, "but I called her last night. Any particular reason you were concerned?"

Maggie hesitated. She was in the position of wanting to find out whatever Pat might know about Kara's relationships, without betraying Kara's confidence. Not only that, but what she really wanted to get around to was possible drug use among the set around Nora. She decided to risk modified frankness. "To be honest," she said, "I'm concerned about Kara and some of the other young people she knows, or may have met through her mother. Her mother was murdered, and I think I know why, but not by whom. I'm afraid some of them—including you, for all I know—may be in danger too."

Might as well hang for a sheep as a lamb, Maggie supposed. And it was true, sort of. She had thought, in general terms, of a possible motive, and if the murder was drug-related, then Kara and/or some of her friends could be threatened. Or, one of them could be the murderer. Maybe even Pat, she realized, as the girl stared at her, open-mouthed.

"I think you know what I mean, Pat," Maggie prompted. "My kids were in high school with Harrison Creitz and Jason Wickers. Are they as much 'fun' as they used to be?"

"Who are you? Are you from the police?" Pat stood as if to leave, scowling down at Maggie.

"No, no," Maggie soothed, her heart in her mouth. "I'm strictly a concerned friend—and a mother."

"I don't know why I should trust you." Pat tossed her head impatiently. As Maggie wondered frantically what else she could say to prolong the interview, the girl suddenly sat down again. "But somehow, I do. And I need to tell someone."

The story Maggie heard in the next hour as the two women walked the flat, tree-lined campus (having left the library for the relative privacy of the great outdoors) included alcohol, sex, and broken hearts a-plenty, as well as a variety of illegal drugs, and would no doubt have shocked the town fathers and the regents of the university. The girl had learned some hard lessons, moving in what passed as a pretty fast crowd in Topeka, Kansas. But none of it offered a motive for Nora Patterson's murder, so far as Maggie could tell.

"So Kara's mother was not supplying anyone with drugs?" she asked Pat, as the younger woman was obviously coming to the end of her sad tale.

"Not that I know of," Pat replied. "What made you think she was?"

"I thought she might be storing drugs in her freezer," Maggie said disingenuously, hoping it sounded true, because it nearly was. "I'm told that pot, LSD, and maybe other things, too, stay fresh longer in cold storage."

"Well, maybe so, but I never knew Nora to have anything but a little grass for her own use. And not even that recently. Everything was clean living and sexual ecstasy. I couldn't go there at all." Pat looked at her watch. "Hey! I've got to run. I've got class. Thanks for listening. Whatever it was killed Nora, I'm pretty sure it wasn't drugs."

"Thank you for talking to me, Pat. And do be careful, won't you?"

Left standing alone under a group of small pine trees near the library, Maggie felt more confused than ever. With no particular goal in mind, she strolled toward the carillon, dodging several hurrying students and a large yellow dog. Nora, it seemed, had indeed found playmates among her daughter's contemporaries, including—Pat had implied without saying it outright—Kara's boyfriend Harrison.

And some of the same young people were involved more or less heavily in the small university's "drug scene." But there was no reason in anything Pat had said to suspect any trafficking on Nora's part. Thus, the idea of the freezer's harboring illicit substances had no basis in fact, so far as Maggie could confirm.

Maggie looked up to find herself at the entry-way to the Memorial Union. Maybe a cup of coffee would help. As she walked through the columned entrance and up the blue-carpeted stairway, Maggie realized she couldn't remember when she had last been in the student union. The cafeteria was closed at this hour, so she bought a cup of coffee from a smiling clerk at the little sundries stand and headed for the "Washburn Room."

Paper cup in hand, she was moving toward an empty table near the wall when she saw a face she recognized on the other side of the large but surprisingly cozy dining room. Lorraine Patterson—what would she be doing on campus, Maggie wondered. She walked over to Lorraine's table. "Mind if I join you?" she asked, her hand on the back of an empty chair.

"What?" Lorraine started, blinked, and looked up at Maggie. Her effort to focus in the here and now was painfully evident.

"You were a million miles away, weren't you, Lorraine?" Maggie offered sympathetically. "Sorry to startle you. May I sit down?"

"Please." Lorraine sounded courteous enough, but her face hadn't quite come back to conventional social mode yet, as she stared wide-eyed at Maggie. "I'm sorry—I know I should know you, but...."

"Maggie Tenwhistle," Maggie said briskly, setting her cup down and extending her hand. "My daughter was in high school with your stepdaughter Kara."

"Oh, of course, Maggie. And you house-sat during the memorial service. Thank you so much, and please do sit down." Lorraine's face had caught up with her voice now, and arranged itself into a pleasant smile as she clasped Maggie's hand warmly and then gestured politely toward the Ichabod-blue plastic chair next to her.

Maggie sat and noticed for the first time the open textbook on the dark plastic-woodgrain table in from of Lorraine. "What are you reading?" she inquired by way of making conversation.

"Anthropology," Lorraine answered. "It's a 100 course, and I'm finding it much less interesting than I thought I would. I suppose one has to learn all the terms and background, but I'd rather read *The Smithsonian* or *Archaeology*."

"Are you working on a degree, or just taking a course?" Maggie asked.

"Oh, I'm hoping to work toward a degree, but I'm just starting here," Lorraine said. "I haven't declared a major yet, and haven't even decided yet what it will be."

"But probably not anthropology?" Maggie guessed.

"Actually, it very well might be. I'm assuming the later courses will be more interesting," Lorraine replied.

Maggie sipped her coffee. It occurred to her that if she had anything useful to learn from Lorraine it would probably not be found discussing anthropology. Having thought she detected a bit of a Southern accent in Lorraine's speech, Maggie tried a ploy she hoped would bring the conversation closer to current events. "You aren't a native Topekan, are you?" she asked hopefully.

"Oh, my, no!" Lorraine sounded surprised. ""I grew up in Texas."

"Well, I would have said 'south of the Mason-Dixon Line,' but I wouldn't have guessed Texas." Maggie was surprised, too.

"My parents were both reared in Alabama," Lorraine explained. "So I've been told before I don't sound like a Texan." Although just then she did, Maggie thought.

"How did you find your way to Kansas?"

"I met Orin when he was on a business trip to Dallas," Lorraine said briefly.

"And he...persuaded you?"

"Persuaded me." Lorraine smiled, her eyes showing an inward look for a moment. Then she seemed almost to shake herself back and looked directly at Maggie. "What are you doing on campus, Maggie? Are you taking classes, too?"

"No, no." Maggie shook her head, scrambling for an answer. ("I was snooping into your extended family's private affairs" didn't seem like a good response!)

"Not yet, anyway. I'd like to, but no, today I was just meeting a friend." This wasn't going her way so far. How could she bring the topic around to Nora without giving Lorraine a reason to just walk away?

Well, the direct approach had worked once today—maybe it would work twice. "Actually, Lorraine, I've been thinking a lot about Nora's death," Maggie said, watching the other woman's face intently. It didn't change, so she plunged on. "I suppose it's rude of me to bring it up, but do you have any idea who might have killed her, or why?"

"Well, it wasn't I, if that's what you mean." Lorraine seemed more amused than offended. "There have been times, mind you, over the past two years," she continued, still speaking lightly. "Nora would phone Orin at home, about the most trivial things. She wouldn't talk to me, even to leave a message. If I answered, she would just hang up. Eventually, she quit calling, at the house." Lorraine stopped speaking abruptly and looked at Maggie, as though daring her to inquire further.

Maggie dared. "You mean she started calling him at work?"

"I think so." And then Lorraine's aplomb suddenly

crumpled. Light blue eyes looked at Maggie from a face that had aged ten years in an instant, as wrinkles and sags invisible a moment ago became all too apparent.

"Do you want to tell me?" Maggie leaned forward encouragingly.

"I think she's been—had been—calling him at his office. His secretary let something slip a couple of months ago. He didn't say anything, and I've been afraid to ask." It came out in a rush, and then Lorraine covered her face with her hands and began to shake with silent sobs.

After a few moments, she stopped shaking. Without raising her head, she fumbled in her purse for a tissue, with which she dabbed daintily at her eyes before straightening. "Pardon me," she said stiffly. "I don't know what caused that outburst."

"It's perfectly all right," Maggie said. She held still, hoping against hope that Lorraine would offer some further explanation.

She didn't. Instead, she began to gather her things from the table. "It's been nice to see you, Maggie. Have a lovely day." Lorraine stood and walked away without a backward glance.

Maggie sat back in her chair, absently draining the last of her lukewarm coffee. What had that been about? Nora had been calling Orin Patterson at his office, and for some reason that upset his present wife. To be sure, most second wives would prefer to forget all about Wife Number One, but Lorraine's reaction seemed out of proportion.

Could it be that Lorraine thought, with or without reason, that Nora was trying to win Orin back? If so, that could give Lorraine a motive for murder. A bit of a stretch, but with both sex and money potentially involved—Orin was certainly both attractive and well-heeled—not too far-fetched, perhaps.

Or maybe Nora's calls were threatening Orin in some way. Did she "have something" on him? Or was he just tired of being pestered? Either way, murder had been committed for less, especially murder of an ex-spouse. Maggie left the Union and walked toward her car, deep in thought.

Without being aware of having made a conscious decision, she found herself driving toward the Friedmanns' house in Potwin, a gracious old Topeka neighborhood that once had been a separate town. The gingerbready two and three-story Victorian houses, bought up and restored by mostly doctors and lawyers in recent decades, continued to comprise one of Topeka's more prestigious areas. As Maggie drove past just-greening lawns, overhung by hundred-year-old oak trees still bare of leaves, three children on bicycles wobbled toward her down the uneven brick street. She pulled over for a moment to let them pass.

The Friedmanns' house was the only one on the block still painted stark white. A few years earlier, architectural historians had proclaimed that the original owners of these homes had most probably enjoyed decorating them in a variety of pastel or brighter colors. Since this discovery, ambitious and sure-handed house painters in Topeka and elsewhere had earned a steady living restoring to former glory many of the centenarian beauties, with as many as fourteen complementary shades designed to bring out all the decorative highlights. Maggie had to admit she liked the colors, sometimes making a game of trying to count the number of hues on a single house—like the one on the corner with blue-gray siding; porch trim of turquoise, navy, and puce; cream, sky blue, and apricot around the windows; and attic trim of navy, cream, and brick.

But the all-white ones still looked proper to her, like the big old houses she'd admired in her home town, growing up. And the house in front of which she parked now looked especially comfortable, with its old-fashioned porch swing now lit by a ray of late-afternoon sun peeking through the trees. Maggie sighed as she switched off the engine and got out of the car. In this peaceful place, she had forgotten for a few moments the puzzle which had been occupying her mind all day.

Buff and Helda not only were at home but seemed delighted to see her. They welcomed her into their rose-carpeted living room, and offered her a seat on a small sofa with flowered upholstery and curved arms of a gleaming wood Maggie guessed was cherry. While Buff engaged Maggie in small talk, Helda disappeared into the kitchen, whence she reappeared shortly with a tray bearing three cups and a small pitcher of cream, along with a sleek European-looking thermal jug.

After pouring the fresh-smelling coffee, Helda offered Maggie a cup and held out the pitcher. "Cream, my dear?" she asked.

"Yes, I believe I will, thanks," Maggie said.

"And you must try some of these," Buff suggested, offering a glass saucer holding small dark-brown balls.

"What are they?" Maggie asked, her hand hovering above the dish.

"Chocolate-covered espresso beans," Buff beamed. "From the Chocolate Bar over your way."

"Oh." Maggie tried to sound more enthusiastic than she felt. She picked up one bean between thumb and forefinger and nibbled it gingerly. Dark chocolate and rich bitter coffee greeted her taste. Not as bad as she'd feared. "I'd better not have any more —caffeine, you know," she said, passing the dish on to Helda, who now sat at her left on the sofa.

Maggie sipped the steaming coffee, and then realized that both of her hosts had fallen silent and were looking at her expectantly. "I guess you're wondering why I'm here," she said, aware she sounded like a B movie cliche. "I'm...not sure myself," she continued, glancing down at the cup in her hand, "but...."

She looked up and saw that Buff and Helda were still sitting quietly, eyes on her face. "Whooh!" she sighed heavily. "Well, the bottom line is, I'm trying to solve Nora's murder. And I'd like to talk with you some more, if you are willing." Maggie laughed nervously and grinned wryly. "So, that's it!"

"Oh, my dear!" Helda reached out to pat Maggie's hand as it lay on the sofa.

"And how can we help?" Buff inquired somberly.

"Maybe first by just listening to what I think I know," Maggie said, greatly relieved that they were neither laughing at her nor trying to talk her out of anything.

Briefly, she reviewed her brief conversation with Lorraine Patterson and her subsequent speculations. "I had been thinking maybe there was a drug connection, but now I'm wondering about Nora's relationship with Orin and his new wife." She looked expectantly at her hosts.

"Orin and Nora's divorce was amicable, so far as I know," Buff said.

"Even though their marriage had not always been so," Helda added. "It is not surprising, however, to learn that Nora would continue to telephone him."

"Nor that she would not want to speak to his new, younger wife." Buff picked up the thread. "She had no reason to be jealous so long as he did not re-marry. But after—yes, I can imagine her wanting to, as they say, 'get her hooks into him' again."

"Would she have had any financial interest?" Maggie wondered aloud.

"Possibly through her girls," Helda volunteered.

"You don't think she was getting child support, surely? Since Kara had been living part of the time with Orin, and more recently in her own apartment? And Karen was long gone," Maggie said.

"Probably not," Buff shook his head. "But maybe alimony."

"In this day and age?" Maggie was doubtful.

"The disparity of income would have been substantial. Sometimes alimony is allowed?" Helda offered.

"But normally only for a few years," Buff supplied.

"Maybe Nora was trying to get him to keep paying," Helda said.

"And he killed her for that?" Buff sounded so incredulous that both Helda and Maggie stared at him. "I mean to say," he hastened to explain, "a powerful lawyer has many options. I doubt he would need to go to such lengths to rid himself of an annoyance."

"Maybe Lorraine, then," Maggie said. "Though I hate to think it of her. She seems nice—very Southern, but still nice."

"Jealousy can be a powerful force," Buff intoned. Maggie hoped he wasn't going into his professorial mode, but he stopped there. The three sat in silence for a moment.

"More coffee, Maggie?" Helda offered.

"No, thanks," Maggie said. "I expect I'd better get going. Thanks for listening."

As she drove away, Maggie realized she really hadn't found out any background on Nora's relationships with other people in the Co-op, especially other men (and their wives, if any). Nor had she asked Buff any weighty psychological questions, like what would be the probable impact on a teenage girl of knowing her mother was bedding her own boyfriend? Or the impact of that situation on the girl's father?

Home early for a change, Maggie decided to cook something substantial. By the time Mike got home, she had made a fair mess of the kitchen, and had chicken-fried steaks sizzling in the skillet and biscuits almost ready to pop in the oven. "Want to get the candlesticks out and have a really romantic dinner?' she asked Mike when he came into the kitchen to say hello.

"Old-fashioned electricity would be good enough for me, but I'll get the candles if you wish," he said.

"Yeah, let's do. For some reason, I feel like it," Maggie said.

After their romantic steak dinner, Mike offered to do the dishes, and then proposed a walk around the block to look at the rising full moon. After that, one thing led to another, and they took full advantage of having the house to themselves.

Leaning back against the pillows several hours later, Mike looked approvingly at his wife. "Mrs. Tenwhistle, if you weren't already married, I'd have to propose to you myself," he said.

"Don't you think your wife would have something to say about that, Mr. Tenwhistle?" Maggie responded, snuggling under his arm.

"Mmmm," Mike said, turning to kiss her once again.

"It's getting late," Maggie said reluctantly, as a yawn caught her unawares, "and I'm getting sleepy." She rolled over and pulled the sheet up.

"You're remembering that I'm taking Geoff to Salina tomorrow, to that Kansas Wesleyan University campus open house," Mike said as he picked up his bedtime book. "I assumed you didn't want to go, but you're welcome, of course."

"Thanks, I know I'm welcome, but I think I just might drive up to Kansas City tomorrow morning myself," Maggie said. How strange! She hadn't known she was planning to do that!

CHAPTER 15

The next morning, Mike's alarm went off at 7:00 as usual. Maggie groaned and rolled over to curl up next to her husband. "I can only cuddle for a minute, Tiger," Mike said softly in her ear. "Geoff and I are going to the open house at Wesleyan, remember?"

"Oh, yeah," Maggie said, suddenly alert. "And I'm going to drive up to Kansas City. Did I tell you that?"

"You said something about it last night. Are you going shopping?" Mike rolled over and out of the bed, with a grunt.

"What do you think?" Maggie said. In the nearly two decades of their marriage, they both knew, Mike could count on the fingers of one hand the number of times Maggie had "gone shopping" as a recreational pastime. "No, I thought I might try to find the lady who hosts those weekend sessions Nora went to, try to find out a little more about them and about Nora. I'm thinking someone she met there must have followed her back to Topeka and—you know."

She climbed out of bed and began to dress in jeans and a long-sleeved cotton shirt of bright blue, topped by a loose-fitting purple t-shirt with "Topeka West" printed in white across the front.

"Tiger," Mike was suddenly very serious. "I won't try to get you to stop what you think you need to do. But be careful. This is a murder, and murders can involve some really nasty folks sometimes. More often than not!"

A few minutes later, Maggie joined Mike and Geoff in the kitchen. Mike poured himself a cup of coffee and popped a couple of slices of toast in the toaster, while Geoff was sitting at the table crafting a delicacy of cheese and tortillas which Maggie understood would soon go into the microwave. "Can I fix my tea first?" she asked, poised cup in hand at the oven door. "Geoff?" she queried when she received no answer, setting her cup into the microwave and keying in the time.

"What? Oh, sure, Mom."

Maggie pushed the start button and the microwave hummed to life. She lifted the Cheerios box from the pantry shelf and poured herself a bowl before sitting down across from her husband, who was now putting slabs of butter on his hot toast. "Did you have good painting last night?" she asked.

"Yeah, we got mostly all done," Geoff replied. "It's going to be awesome. All bright reds, yellows, and greens. Like an Abstract Expressionist painting. Really different. You guys have a good evening?"

"Mmmhmm," Maggie nodded, her mouth full of cereal. Mike just smiled.

The microwave sounded to signal its readiness for another job, and Geoff stood up. He handed his mother her tea and began microwaving his quesadilla.

"You were very quiet coming in last night," Maggie said conversationally, pouring milk into her tea. "At least I didn't hear you. What time did you get home?"

"Dad was still up," Geoff replied.

"He was punctual, as usual," Mike confirmed. Geoff joined his parents at the table and began to slather his steaming quesadilla with picante sauce.

"Don't hassle the lad," Mike said to Maggie a few minutes later, after Geoff had excused himself to get ready to go to the university open house. "He's never given us cause to doubt him."

"I know," Maggie said. "And he's about to go off on his own. I know, I know! It's seeing all these other kids who have messed themselves up so badly. It makes me mother-hennish, that's all."

"All what other kids?" Mike asked, going to pour himself

another cup of coffee.

"I talked with one of Kara Patterson's friends yesterday." Maggie stood and began to clear the table. "I just heard a lot about how out of control some young people are these days, that's all." And, Officer Mike, she thought, you don't really want to hear the details or you might have to do something about it.

As if he had heard her thoughts, Mike said quietly, "There's only so much parents or even the law can do to protect kids. At some point, they make their choices and they have to…"

He broke off as Geoff came bounding down the stairs. "Ready to go, Dad?" he called.

"I know you're right," Maggie said softly, for Mike's ears only. "But it still makes me scared for them"

"Yo!" Mike answered Geoff. "Go on out, I'm coming." He leaned over to kiss Maggie. "You okay, Little Woman?"

"Just fine. You drive carefully, and have a good time. What time will you be home?"

"In time for dinner, I guess," Mike said. "If we're going to be later than 6:30, we'll call. Okay?" Maggie nodded. "You drive carefully, too. And don't get into any trouble in the big city." He shook his finger close to her face.

"No, Sir," Maggie answered in mock military fashion, and then grabbed his finger and kissed it with a loud wet smack. "Off you go, you two. Have fun!" She shooed Mike out the door and stood in the doorway watching as her menfolk drove off. Her heart filled with gratitude for the blessings of her family. They'd be fine, knock on wood. Maggie tapped the door jamb with her knuckles, and turned back into the house.

It looked like a beautiful day. After washing up the breakfast dishes, Maggie changed into a dark cotton skirt that reached nearly to her ankles. She topped it with a long-sleeved green shirt and slipped a pair of silver and amber earrings into her ears. She brushed her hair and twirled in front of the mirror. Not bad, she thought, taking a bright yellow denim jacket out of the closet.

Then she made herself a second cup of tea and began to think about her contemplated trip. The logical thing to do would be to call this Kathy Gegeshina to see if she was going to be home, before driving the sixty miles to Kansas City. Maggie hunted for, and found, the notes she had taken from Nora's house, and started to punch in the number listed for "Kathy." She paused, and then clicked the off button on the phone, and sat down on the sofa, an attentive look coming over her face.

She really wanted just to drive to Kansas City without calling ahead, she realized. It didn't make good sense, but it felt right. It could be a waste of gas, but on the other hand, it was a beautiful day for a drive, anyway. And what if this Kathy wouldn't want to see her? What could Maggie say over the phone to convince her? "My neighbor has been murdered and I want to come see if you or one of your friends might have done it?"

Not a good plan. If she just showed up, and the woman was there, Maggie would probably at least get inside. At the worst, she'd have a lovely drive, get a look at the outside of the house, have a nice lunch in Westport or the Plaza, and drive home again.

Having talked herself into the rationality of her intuitive preference, Maggie realized she had no idea of where Kathy Gegeshina lived, except that it was "in Kansas City." Stymied for a moment, she was almost ready to phone after all when she realized that, if she were lucky, the greater Kansas City phone book would have the address. Even if the phone was listed under Ms. Gegeshina's husband's name (assuming she had a husband) or under initials, Maggie could cross-check since she had a phone number that was presumably correct.

It took only a few minutes' phone conference with a friendly reference librarian at the Topeka Public Library to locate and confirm an address in the western suburb of Mission, Kansas, for "M. K. Gegeshina." A few minutes later, Maggie had gassed up her Datsun and was heading for the Kansas turnpike.

It was indeed a beautiful day, the big prairie sky a glorious clear azure and the roadsides just beginning to show green through the dead remains of the previous year. Maggie clicked on her favorite public radio station to listen to a Saturday morning jazz program. Easing up the volume on her "not-half-bad sound system," she pounded the steering wheel happily to the rhythm of "In the Mood" as she sped east through the increasingly wooded hills toward Kansas City.

Once in the metro area, it didn't take long to find the street in the historic suburb of Mission where Kathy Gegeshina's cottage was located. After turning right at the red brick buildings of the Methodist Indian Mission for which the town had been named, Maggie soon came across Elmwood Street. A few minutes later she was pulling up in front of the house designated on the slip of paper she'd brought from home.

The small frame bungalow was an astonishment of bright apricot, with white shutters and turquoise trim on the porch supports. Copper wind chimes with a soft blue-green patina hung under the porch roof, along with a large wood-feather-and-string "spider web" creation that Maggie recognized as an Ojibway dream catcher. The short curve of a flagstone walk was lined with intensely-yellow daffodils. Approaching the house between the undulating yellow bonnets, Maggie noted with agreeable surprise that spring here was a few days advanced as compared with Topeka. Just in front of the low porch, an assortment of tulips stood in varying degrees of bud and near-bloom, with dark purple grape hyacinths clustered near the steps.

As Maggie knocked on the old but neatly-painted wood-framed screen door, she noticed a beautiful fanlight above the door, jewel tones of red and blue glowing in combination with clear and frosted glass in an old-fashioned pattern. Kathy Gegeshina evidently had a love of both the antique and the colorful, at least in exterior decoration.

When the door opened, it was obvious the preference for the unusual did not stop at the threshold. The middle-aged face that looked out at Maggie was lined and conventionally

Midwestern-looking, but the costume that went with it was fresh, flowing, and anything but conventional. A bright gold, green, and pink gown (Maggie supposed you could call it a caftan) of some kind of shiny material was topped with a short cape of dark blue fur. A heavy gold chain held the cape in place, and a gold turban allowed only a few wisps of faded brown hair to escape. A large hand with several gold rings on long graceful fingers reached for the screen, but did not open it.

"Yes?" the woman inquired.

Maggie threw out a quick visualization for centering and protection from any unwanted energies. "Good morning," she said. "I'm Maggie Tenwhistle, from Topeka. Are you Kathy Gegeshina?"

"Yes, I am," the woman said, in a deep, pleasant tone. "What can I do for you?"

"I think you know, or used to know, Anna Prince, and maybe Suzanne Coffey? They're friends of mine, in Topeka."

"Certainly I know Anna and Suz. How do you come to know them?" The woman's hand rested on the frame of the screen door, but as yet she had not pushed it open.

Understanding that she was being screened as surely as if she'd been asked to produce an I.D. card, Maggie nodded. "I can't actually remember how I met them, but we've been in a tarot group together, along with Laurie Jetts, for more than five years.

"And of course, we work in the co-op together. I was house-sitting for the Patterson family yesterday, but I understand you sang at the memorial service for Nora." There, she'd shot her wad. If the woman was going to let her in, it would have to be now. Maggie willed a smile on her face and tried to still her right hand which seemed to be trembling a bit.

"Of course. I saw Anna there. Come in—Maggie, was it? Welcome to my home." Kathy Gegeshina swung the door wide, and stood back, ushering Maggie in with a sweeping gesture.

Inside, the house was almost as unusual as it was outside. Large vines and other houseplants filled every corner of the small living room and climbed around the lace-curtained windows. A braided rug in rusts, blues, and ivories coiled in a large oval in the center of the room, covering most of a varnished wood floor. Light-colored walls were hung with bright scarves, primitive-looking wooden masks and carved sticks, and several professional quality nature photographs in wooden frames. A small crystal ball stood in a golden cradle on a low bookcase near one window.

The glimpse Maggie caught of the kitchen showed an avocado-colored refrigerator and the corner of a plain wooden table, a half-open pantry, and dull-looking vinyl flooring of a nondescript color.

"Won't you sit down?" her hostess invited, indicating a dark red overstuffed sofa of a certain age. "Can I get you something to drink, some tea or coffee?"

"Oh, no thanks," Maggie said, "although, actually, I'd love a glass of plain tap water if it's no trouble."

"No trouble at all," Kathy said. "I'm a water drinker myself." She disappeared through the open doorway into the kitchen, while Maggie seated herself on the sofa. Or more precisely, as she sank into the sofa. She wondered whether she would be able to stand up again without help. Might as well relax and enjoy for now.

When Kathy returned, she had a glass of water in each hand. She gave one to Maggie and seated herself in a wood rocking chair which she pulled across the rug till it was quite close to where Maggie half-reclined in the soft sofa. "So what brings you to Mission?" Kathy asked, her keen eyes seeming to look into Maggie's thoughts.

Surmising this was not a woman to trifle with, Maggie decided her best approach was overt frankness. "I am trying to find out more about Nora Patterson. A friend of mine may be accused of her murder, and I'm trying to learn something that will suggest who really did it. I hoped maybe you could tell me something that would help. If you're willing to talk about her, that is." Maggie thought she noticed a hint of some emotion passing across the other woman's face, but it was so fleeting she had no chance of identifying it.

"Of course, I've known Nora for years," Kathy said. "Recently she's been coming to sessions once a month with Baba Sin De; however, I knew her and Orin and the girls when I lived in Lawrence. But no doubt you know that." She looked at Maggie as though challenging her to be more specific.

"Could you tell me a little bit about what Baba Sin De's weekend sessions are like? Or is that privileged information?" Maggie asked.

"It's not secret, but it is a little hard to explain. We do group meditations and guided imagery, but with Baba's energy he's able to lead us into states which would be difficult or impossible to achieve alone," Kathy said. "Unless you've experienced it, it really is hard to understand. It's quite intense, especially the Saturday and Sunday sessions. The Friday night introductory part is more for the general public."

"When Nora was here, did anything strange happen? Or was anybody…did she interact with anyone in a way that might have led to conflict?" Maggie wished she'd thought out how to pursue this line of questioning.

"Strange things are always happening whenever Baba is around," Kathy said. "People go into trance, we laugh, cry, dance, yell. It's impossible to predict from one minute to the next what is going to happen."

"Well, this last weekend—did anything special happen with Nora? Obviously, I'm thinking of anything that might bear on what happened when she got back to Topeka that Sunday. Did she meet anyone new, did anyone argue with her or seem especially interested in her?" Maggie felt frustrated by the fact that she didn't know exactly what she was looking for and was dependent on Kathy to decide what incident or behavior might be relevant.

Kathy looked at Maggie with a puzzled frown and cocked her head to one side. "I don't understand. You're talking about this past weekend, Friday, March 15th?"

"Yes," Maggie said. Now she was puzzled.

"But Nora wasn't here last weekend. The only person here from Topeka was Leslie Stone."

"But she rode up with Les. She must have been here," Maggie protested before she could stop herself.

"These gatherings are not so large that I don't know who is in my house," Kathy said with quiet dignity. "Nora was definitely not here."

"But," Maggie said, "Les was going to bring her, I'm sure of that." At least she had thought she was sure.

"I didn't hear it myself," Kathy said, "but I believe Les told someone Nora didn't answer the door when he called for her at the agreed-upon time."

"Did you tell the police this?" Maggie asked, her mind whirling.

"I told them Les was here from late Friday evening to afternoon on Sunday, around 3:00 or 3:30. They didn't ask about Nora." Kathy looked keenly at Maggie. "Does this make a difference?"

"I don't know," Maggie said. "It might. It's just so unexpected." Why hadn't Les told her Nora didn't go to Kansas City? He'd had numerous opportunities to do so. She felt a bit light-headed, and took a sip water to cover her confusion.

"Did Nora and Les normally come together? I mean, was that their regular pattern?" she asked.

"Sometimes they came together, sometimes not. Sometimes other people came from Topeka. There might be several cars from there, or from Lawrence. This time Les happened to be the only one. I didn't think anything about it."

"What did you understand their relationship to be? Les and Nora? Were they lovers?" Maggie suddenly felt an inclination to pursue the matter with this strong and perceptive woman.

"Lovers?" Kathy echoed, her mellow voice seeming to carry

a hint of laughter. "Oh, no, I'm quite certain not."

"If you don't mind my asking, how are you so certain? By the way they acted together?"

"They don't, didn't 'act together' much at all, so far as that goes," Kathy answered. "They sometimes drove here together, but one didn't think of them as being 'together' once they were here. Nora was, shall I say, quite active, with other men in the group. My sense is that's why her daughter didn't come back after her first visit."

"And Les, he didn't seem to be jealous or otherwise bent out of shape?" Maggie was struggling to make sense of Les's behavior.

"I wouldn't have said so. But then I wouldn't have been looking for anything like that. Nora was quite sexual, as you no doubt know, and she was always 'on.'" Kathy had the inward look of a person trying to call up from the past details which had seemed of no significance at the time. "I'd say there was some degree of sexual tension between them, Nora being what she was. And Les's celibacy being clearly a discipline, not a natural gift. But lovers, no. I think not."

"Les is celibate? Some kind of monk?" Maggie felt confused. "Is this some kind of religion?"

"I'm surprised you wouldn't know, if you know Les at all well, " Kathy said, smiling. "No, celibacy isn't common practice among our group, but Les seems to feel it is a calling for him. He talks about it a lot in the group, and I know Baba has been working with him. That's why I wouldn't expect him to be reacting to someone like Nora, at least not openly."

Afterward, Maggie didn't recall thanking Kathy Gegeshina, leaving the pink house, or driving from Mission to the famous Country Club Plaza. She barely remembered having lunch at Houlihans. On the way home, she was still trying to make sense of what Kathy had told her. Assuming Les and Nora were not intimate, as the very astute Ms. Gegeshina felt sure they were not, then it seemed unlikely that Les, living way out in Auburn, would have a key to Nora's house.

And lacking access to the house, he didn't seem to be a viable suspect. So why had Les lied to Maggie about taking Nora to Kansas City? For he clearly had deceived her, if not by commission then certainly by omission. And why did no one else, not even Sondra, seem to know Nora had not gone to K.C.? Or did Sondra know Nora had been at home (or at least not in Kansas City) all day Saturday and Sunday—in which case why was *she* lying to Maggie (and presumably to the police also)?

What had Nora been doing and whom had she seen during those two days? Maggie felt as though she had been tricked into barking up the wrong tree, wasting a great deal of precious time. She pictured herself on all fours, barking frantically around the base of a leafless tree while Nora sat laughing, screened by thick greenery, in the branches of another tree nearby.

Another image floated into Maggie's mind, as her car sped along the four-lane highway. It was a crystal bowl tipping over and spilling out apples, grapes, and oranges onto a white plastic ground cover of some kind. A dream image, she thought, from a couple of days ago maybe. What was it trying to remind her of?

Nora's eating habits, her fruit and nut diet, encouraged if not suggested by the remarkable and mysterious Baba Sin De? In the dream, she remembered, the bowl had been shattered by a shot, or at least a loud noise. That seemed to have some relevance, but didn't tell Maggie anything she didn't already know.

She pictured again Nora laughing at her from among the green leaves. Then for some reason, she thought of the dry leaves in Nora's compost pile: all those leaves Nora had apparently raked up just before she died, and the odd white layer just below them. Suddenly Maggie knew what that white-white reminded her of. Freezer paper! The kind of freezer paper in which Nora's nuts and some of her dried fruits had been packaged, those dozens of packages and cartons of food which had been conspicuously absent by the night after Nora's death.

Had Nora emptied her freezer so hurriedly that she didn't bother to unwrap anything?

Maggie broke off her reverie as she approached the West Topeka turnpike exit. She paid the toll, and drove the few blocks to her home still puzzling over what intuition told her was a connection that must be made between Nora's death and the empty freezer chest. And why had Les let Maggie believe Nora had gone with him to Kansas City?

CHAPTER 16

Arriving home, Maggie unlocked the door and stepped inside with a sigh. She felt as though she had already worked a long day, even though it was only 2:00, and a Saturday at that. She dropped her bag and draped her jacket over the stair railing. She'd hang it up in a little while, she promised herself. Right now she needed to sit down with a cup of tea and think about nothing.

She walked down the three wide steps to the main floor, aware that something besides physical tiredness was bothering her. This business with Nora must be getting to her nerves. In the kitchen, she filled a cup with water, dropped in a tea bag, and set the microwave for two and a half minutes, her hands working habitually while her mind was struggling to analyze the growing sense of unease she felt.

Her arms and the back of her neck prickled, as though the hairs were standing up. If the door hadn't been locked when she came in, she'd have sworn someone else was in the house. She wandered back into the living room, still focused on the strange inner sensations.

The first thing Maggie noticed out of place was the stack of newspapers. Instead of being in a loose pile beside Mike's chair where they habitually landed each morning, the papers were stacked neatly in front of the television set. Then Maggie noticed that her tarot cards, which she was certain she had left in their lidded box, were spread across the sofa. More curiously, all of the cards were face down, except for two in the center, which were face up. Moving closer, Maggie saw that of the two face-up cards, one depicted a serenely-smiling person hanging head-down from a leafless tree, while the other showed the image of a skeleton crowned with black thorns and leaning on a large sickle —"The Hanged Man" and "Death."

In spite of herself, Maggie shivered. Someone *had* been in the house. But Mike and Geoff couldn't be back in town yet, and Alyssa was more than a hundred miles away at college. Unless— it must have been Alyssa, Maggie told herself firmly. And if she'd been and gone, she'd have left a note on the board.

Maggie half-ran to the kitchen to check the small metal board by the phone that served as the family message center. Two hours away at school, Alyssa had always honored her parents' request that she leave word if she'd been in the house unannounced. But this time there was no note.

She forgot—or she figured she'd be right back, and didn't bother, Maggie tried to believe. But the warning clangs of her own nerves belied this easy comfort. Well, she'd just call Alyssa's residence hall room. If she got her roommate, she could ask where Alyssa was, and if not, at least she could leave a message on the machine.

After just two rings, however, a familiar voice answered. "Alyssa?" Maggie asked, hoping against hope that it wasn't.

"Hi, Mom," the voice said cheerily. "How you doin'?"

"Okay. Actually, not so well right now. I think our house has been burglarized. Or, I guess I don't know. But someone has been in here. I think I'm going to search the rest of the house. Do you have time to talk to me while I do, so I won't be so scared? I'll turn the phone here up as high as it will go and then grab the one in the bedroom when I get up there. Do you have time to do that?"

Alyssa's "Sure, Mom. But be careful!" sounded rather faintly from the kitchen phone as Maggie tiptoed up the stairs to the second floor. She entered the master bedroom and moved quickly to grab the phone there from its cradle. "Can you hear me?" she asked, after laying the receiver on the bed.

"I hear you." Alyssa's voice came now in stereo. Maggie

turned to open the doors of first her closet and then Mike's. "As though anyone really could hide in these tiny closets," she said, raising her voice. "But I wouldn't feel safe if I didn't check." She shoved the closet doors shut and left the bedroom.

Moving next to Geoff's room, she swung open the door wide, and after a pause, stepped in, pushing the door firmly all the way against the wall. She reached gingerly for the door to the closet, loudly describing her action to Alyssa as she did so. She jerked the closet door open and peered inside. Bending down, she peeked under Geoff's bed before realizing that with all the sports equipment and other assorted stuff he had stored there, no one larger than a baby could possibly have found space to hide.

"Now your room," she shouted to Alyssa, moving to open the door to what would become a "spare room" in just a few short years, once Alyssa was permanently out on her own.

Maggie looked around her daughter's bedroom, with its dark green and cream wallpaper and framed music and drama posters over the abandoned-looking bed. As she repeated the closet inspection, she heard Alyssa speak again: "Has anything been taken, Mom?"

"I haven't noticed anything yet," Maggie said. "The tv, stereo, and microwave are all in place. Nothing seems to have been touched in your room, and I wouldn't be able to tell if Geoff's room had been trashed anyway." She heard Alyssa's chuckle as she completed her survey of the upstairs by a quick glance into the bathroom.

After hanging up the phone in her bedroom, Maggie hurried down the stairs, her heart still pounding. "I'm going to check the downstairs bathroom and laundry room," she told Alyssa-on-the-kitchen-phone, "and then I can breathe again. This reminds me of when I was a girl at home alone. I'd hear noises in that old house and have to go from room to room, upstairs and down, checking everywhere as fast as I could, before I'd feel comfortable and able to go on with whatever I was doing.

"Well, nobody downstairs either. And nothing missing that I can see. Even your dad's change jar is untouched."

"So, Mom, if you don't mind my asking, what makes you think someone's been in the house?" Alyssa asked.

"Oh, I didn't say, did I? Things in the living room are moved around from when I left this morning. Your dad and Geoff left for Salina an hour before I started out, and I'm reasonably sure they aren't back yet."

"Was the door open?"

"No, that's the odd thing. It was locked when I got home. Otherwise, I'd think some kids had gotten in and played a prank." Maggie walked around the house once more, wiggling window frames and checking on the back patio door. All were tightly locked. She returned to the kitchen, reset the volume on the phone and raised it to her ear.

"You know, Alyssa, I think someone got in somehow and left these few changes just to scare me."

"Mom, this isn't good. Should you get someone else over there?" Alyssa sounded concerned.

"Oh, I'm sure it's just a prank," Maggie said firmly. If she couldn't convince herself, at least she could reassure her daughter. "Maybe I left the door unlocked, and someone came in while I was gone and just locked it when they went out again to mystify us."

"Well, I hope you find out who it was," Alyssa said. She sounded relieved. "I don't like the idea of someone being in the house while nobody's home."

"You and me both," Maggie said. "It feels really creepy. So how is everything with you?" she asked, changing the subject.

"Pretty okay. Busy, busy, of course. My choir has a series of concerts next weekend, and that means trying to get some work done ahead. Music Composition is really fun, but it takes lots of hours. More like a lab than a regular class."

"Are you liking what you are producing?"

"Some of it. Some of it is pretty banal. I'll have to bring

some of it home and play it for you."

"I'd like that. I need to try to keep up with you at least a little bit," Maggie said. Her daughter's interest in and talent for music was a source of pride but also of misgivings, as Maggie struggled to understand the dissonant sounds that passed for contemporary music. She tried to keep an open mind, but truth to tell, she didn't like most of it very much, and she feared her lack of comprehension would become a barrier between her and Alyssa. "Well, I expect I'd better let you go. Thanks for holding my hand," she said.

"Glad you called, Mom. Are you sure you're okay now?" the younger woman asked. "Should you call the police?" Now her questions sounded less anxious, more routine.

"And tell them my tarot cards have been messed with?" Maggie laughed. "Can you imagine what your dad would have to put up with from his buddies if I did that? No, I'm sure it's okay. Probably just someone's idea of a joke. Don't think anything more about it. I'm not going to. Bye-bye, dear. Thanks again, and have a good weekend."

"Bye, Mom. Thanks for calling."

But Maggie did think more about it. She set the phone down and walked into the living room to study the upturned tarot cards. It couldn't have been the cat, she admitted. So someone had deliberately put those cards that way.

If it was meant to scare her, it had been done by someone with only cursory knowledge of the tarot. Anyone who worked with the cards, or even had read much about them, would have known that the Hanged Man traditionally symbolized not "hanging" but a complex sort of "doing your own thing" or "joyous sacrifice for a higher good."

And the Death card, while very archetypal and strong, seldom represented actual physical death, of the querent or anyone else. An experienced reader like Maggie learned to welcome, rather than fear, the appearance in a layout of the Death card, with its implications of change and opportunities for re-creation.

So if they meant to scare her—well, they'd succeeded, but not on the occult level. And as for the newspapers—was that deliberate, too, Maggie wondered? She picked up the top paper and studied it. It was the front section of the morning's *Kansas City Star*, and the lead story was of the disappearance of a second socially-prominent woman in as many days from an upper middle-class KC suburb. No evidence of foul play had been found in either case, but police were investigating and the community was "alarmed."

Coincidence that this was the item uppermost in the stack of papers? Or another deliberate scare tactic? Maggie told herself she had no rational way of knowing. But she also had to admit that her emotions were in such turmoil she couldn't rely on her usually sound intuition for any help.

Remembering her tea, she went to the kitchen, removed the tea bag from the now-lukewarm tea, and punched the "instant minute" button on the microwave for a quick warm-up. She'd drink her tea, and then try to meditate for a bit and see if she could get clear-headed.

Twenty minutes later, though much calmer than before, Maggie concluded she was still too jangled to be able to think or "know" with clarity what was happening. She picked up the phone again and dialed a familiar number. "Suz," she said in a moment, "I need some help. Are you busy this afternoon?" She paused, listening.

"Well, I'd like to convene an emergency meeting of the Tuesday Night Club, if people can come. Would you want to call Anna while I call Laurie, and whoever can come, show up at my house as soon as possible?"

After another pause, she continued, "I'd rather not say. Nothing life-threatening, but I'd like to get your takes unprejudiced by what I think. Okay, then, come on over when you can. I'll put on hot water." She laughed shortly. "Bye-bye.

Thanks."

Maggie reached Laurie with ease, and gave her virtually the same non-explanation, receiving the same reassuring response. It was great to have such friends, Maggie thought, as she filled the tea-kettle.

Within fifteen minutes, the four women were seated on the floor in Maggie's living room, looking at the "evidence" in the form of the newspaper and the spread-out Tarot cards.

"No, Maggie," Suz said with a sober face, "this was definitely not done by the cat!"

"I was afraid you'd say that," Maggie said, attempting lightness.

"Somebody wanted to make a point with you, I'd say," Anna commented, studying the newspaper article. "This news story could have been on top by coincidence, but if so, why did they move the newspapers at all? Nothing else was bothered?"

"Not that I can tell. The cat's toy mouse might be under a different chair, but I don't count that."

"And nothing is missing? Did you look at the family silver?" Laurie asked.

"This family doesn't have any real silver," Maggie smiled. "But no, I can't find anything missing, and yes, I did check the few transportable valuables we have—Mother's diamond, Mike's stamp collection. Not even the dust is disturbed."

"Well, if we were to read the cards here, I'd say you were looking at dramatic change and the opportunity to sacrifice comfort for some cause you value," Susanna said. "Are you anticipating anything like this in the near future, Maggie?"

"I don't know. Not anticipating, no." Maggie's smile was a bit forced.

"You're holding out on us, Maggie," Anna said. "What's eating you?"

"Well, I..." Maggie hesitated, remembering the cards from the night before with their warning about keeping her own counsel. "I've been thinking a lot about Nora's murder and trying to puzzle out who could have been involved," she said finally.

"Okay, don't tell us if you don't want to," Anna said. "Just remember you don't fool us. We know you too well."

"I...thanks, if you don't mind. Later, maybe, for sure." Maggie shrugged guiltily, telling herself that while she didn't really mistrust her friends, there was no sense involving them in something that might be turning out to be dangerous.

"We could do a layout on this break-in, if you like," Laurie suggested, looking at Maggie.

"Mmhm. Yes, I think that's a good idea," Maggie said, relieved they were not going to push her any more for the moment. "The question could be 'what would it help me to know about the intrusion into my house?' Somebody else want to do it? I'm just not feeling real centered right now."

"Understandable," Laurie remarked drily. "Here, I'll do it. Shall I use your cards, since they're out?"

Maggie nodded.

Laurie shuffled expertly, cut the deck, and selected a stack from which she proceeded to deal the customary eleven-card spread. The first card dealt was the same one Maggie had gotten the night before, the Queen of Swords with her soaring white bird. Maggie stared at it, her mind going back to the image of Nora as the Ice Queen.

Suddenly, she got to her feet. "You go ahead and finish it without me," she told her surprised friends. I'll be right back. There's something I just have to confirm."

She flew up the stairs to the landing, grabbed her jacket from where it still lay over the railing, and hurried out the front door before anyone could ask her any questions.

Outside, she threaded her way between the carport and the next-door neighbors' house, making her way to the little-used alley that ran for several blocks between the houses on the east side of Yew Street and those on the west side of Oak.

When she reached the Patterson property line, she was out of breath, but she quickly unlatched the back gate and ran directly to the compost bin. Wishing she had brought a rake or spading fork, she gingerly pulled aside the soggy layer of leaves to reveal a mound of bulky white paper packages, interspersed with plastic freezer boxes. Though blotched with leaf stain, some of the packages were still identifiable from smeared labels reading "dried peaches," "walnut pieces," and, generically, "NUTS." There could be no question what they were. And moreover, Maggie thought she knew why they were there.

Under normal circumstances, no serious composter would have put anything out that way, and if only by virtue of having a fancy compost bin in her suburban backyard, Nora herself had to be reckoned a serious composter. Nora the Ice Queen, the middle-aged sexpot, the spiritual seeker—Maggie thought of the Queen of Swords standing on her snowy hillside, pointing to her snowy owl. Nora who had *not* gone to Kansas City as planned but stayed in Topeka and done what?—until Sunday evening, when somebody came to the door, took her own gun, and shot her.

And then emptied her freezer? And took the stuff out to the compost pile in the rain? Must have been a pretty good reason to want to get to the bottom of that freezer, if the murderer stayed around to do it while Nora's body lay there getting stiff in the next room.

Less than five minutes later, Maggie was back, seated with her friends in her living room. "I want to go back to the spread I did Wednesday night about the turtle vibes," Maggie said. "It occurs to me that the turtle was in the house—in Nora's house, I mean—last weekend when Nora was killed, and I think there is a connection."

Well, that much was true. So what if she wasn't being entirely frank about what the connection was. Laurie tilted her head quizzically and looked at Maggie with an expression of exaggerated skepticism, but no one said anything; they all nodded in unison when Maggie asked if they were through with the layout they had just done.

Consulting her notebook, Maggie selected and laid out the cards as they had been three days earlier. "Okay," she said, "here's the Five of Swords—'this helps me'—arguably this was telling us back then that we were dealing with a murder. And the lovely, dancing World in her cheerful colors—'this crosses.' Trying to be 'Mrs. Nice Guy' is not going to help solve the problem. Going toward the nightmare, Nine of Swords, but in the middle of the nightmare is also the key. I think that refers to this present business. I think it *is* meant as a threat, but I need to press on through, looking for the key, rather than try to get out of it. Do you think I'm over-dramatizing?' Maggie stopped and looked at each of her friends in turn.

Finally Suz spoke. "No, Maggie, I guess I don't think you are over-dramatizing. It seems clear to me that someone was trying to frighten you, and if you are poking around trying to find out who killed Nora Patterson, then it's reasonable to suppose that has something to do with the person who broke into your house. Does Mike know what you are doing? And where is Mike, by the way?"

"He's on his way home, I hope, he and Geoff, from Salina."

"Maggie, the reading we did while you ran out said essentially the same thing," Laurie said. "That you were involved in something dangerous, something involving death and some pretty powerful emotions."

"And that, while you could find the way through, you were putting yourself in jeopardy by the way you were going about it." Anna reached over and put her hand on Maggie's shoulder. "We'd like to help, or talk you into being more careful, or something. Really, you have talked to Mike about what you are doing?"

"Sort of," Maggie said, ducking her head apologetically. "He says the same thing, 'Be careful.' But after this, if I tell him about it, he may say more than that!"

"Not that I'd blame him," Suz said drily.

"I want to look at the rest of this reading," Maggie said. "Remember this one? The Devil, with the people chained together up and down the steps? Nora seems to have stirred up a lot of conflicts over who belongs to whom, and maybe who has power over whom. Her ideas along these lines were, to say the least, unconventional."

No one else said anything, but all three heads were nodding. Maggie continued. "I've been told that Nora may have been sleeping with her daughter Kara's boyfriend, a kid young enough to be her son! And probably with that other young man who was at Sondra's yesterday—Jason somebody. And who knows how many men in the group she went to in K.C."

"I'd be really surprised if Nora were sleeping with Jas." Suz frowned, as though concentrating hard.

"Me too," Anna said. "I should think he has his—shall we say, his hands—full, with Sondra."

"Sondra and Jas? Don't tell me!" Maggie grimaced. "Why didn't she say that when I asked who Jas was?"

"Probably because she thought you'd disapprove, which obviously you would have," Laurie pointed out.

"Well, suppose Nora was bedding Jason as well as Kara's boyfriend," Anna began, and then stopped. "What makes you think she was involved with Kara's boyfriend?"

"For one thing, the song you said he sang at the memorial service," Maggie said. "The love song?"

"Oh, that was Kara's boyfriend?" Anna was surprised. "Well, yes, now that you mention it, I guess it was quite personal. So, if she was 'seeing' both of these young men, that gives several people possible motives of jealousy, wouldn't you think?"

"Including Sondra," Laurie said.

The three Gang members departed soon thereafter, amid reciprocal offers of further aid and promises to seek aid in event of need. Once again alone in the house, Maggie found she couldn't settle down. She brewed a another mug of tea in the microwave, pacing from sink to table to window and back again until the buzzer sounded. Then, cup in hand, she wandered from room to room, staring at familiar furnishings with the eyes of a stranger. Her house, which had always been her haven, so sunny and safe, now felt alien. It was true what they said about break-ins. "Violated" was not too strong a word. Even the tea she sipped absently seemed to have an unpleasant, metallic taste.

If somebody connected with Nora's death had been in the house, that meant Maggie's curiosity was perceived as a threat to that somebody. But who knew she was even poking around? Besides Mike and Geoff, of course, and the Gang. Oh, and Sondra. And Les Stone, she supposed, maybe, and the Friedmanns, for sure, but they certainly were safe.

Who else? Carl, she smiled to herself. And he certainly wasn't too happy about her curiosity, but he also didn't need to break into her house to make that clear! What about Orin Patterson? How snoopy had she sounded that day on the stairs at Sondra's flood? And who might have overheard her talking with Buff and Helda in the kitchen. Kara? Jas? Harrison Creitz? They had all been there, along with Orin when Maggie had blundered on about access and keys. And one or all of them could very well have such access to Nora's house.

Maggie shivered. Someone had access to her house, too!

CHAPTER 17

By the time Mike and Geoff got home, Maggie had picked up the newspapers and put away her cards, and had a simple supper laid out. Over the meal, Geoff was bubbling with excitement about the drama and history departments at the university they had visited. Afterward, Mike and Maggie washed up together, and Maggie told Mike about her trip to Kansas City. Having decided to avoid mention of the intrusion into their home, she summed up for him the information she had gathered and the conclusions she'd reached since she'd last seen him nearly twelve hours earlier.

"So, it seems to me that I should be looking for people with a good alibi for Sunday night, but no alibi for Friday night and/or Saturday. I don't see any way to tell which time she really was murdered—could have been any time before Sunday night, depending on how long she was in the freezer. My best guess would be Friday night after Kara left, just because nobody seems to have seen Nora since—she didn't answer when Les came to get her, and she had given no hint she wasn't going with him. But the official investigators won't have any more certain idea than I, because the body was cremated. Did you know that?"

"I guess I did," Mike said. "At least, it doesn't surprise me."

"Mike, would you call Carl Nelson and see what news you can pick up?" Maggie asked. "I would think they might check the inside of the freezer and find out the body had been in it. That at least might be worth something."

"Maggie, honey, I don't mind calling Carl, but this freezer business sounds pretty tenuous to me," Mike said.

"But it's obvious a careful gardener like Nora would never have put all that paper and cardboard in her compost pile." Mike looked doubtful. "Well, she wouldn't!" Maggie said emphatically. "It's probably plastic-coated. It'd take ages to decay, even the paper part, and would foul up the balance in the pile completely.

"Besides," she added when Mike continued to frown skeptically, "there were even some plastic cartons. Anyone, no matter how dumb they were about composting, would know that plastic cartons weren't biodegradable. It seems pretty unmistakable to me that the freezer was cleaned out by someone who was in a huge hurry and didn't want to attract attention by having trash bags sitting around. You could at least mention it to him," Maggie pleaded.

"If it will keep you from poking around any more by yourself, I certainly will mention it," Mike agreed.

In the event, Mike didn't mention the freezer to Carl after all. Instead, the phone conversation he reported to Maggie a few minutes later centered around Carl's prediction that the M squad was just about ready to arrest Sondra.

Maggie was incredulous. "How can they be so sure?" she demanded. "Why do they suspect Sondra—why not Orin, or Lorraine, or Les Stone—he was probably the last one to see her alive, even by their theory of the time of death."

"They all have alibis," Mike explained patiently. "Orin and Lorraine and Kara were all three together all evening on Sunday, and Les was working at the co-op, with Suz and that Kit woman you dislike so much. But, Maggie, you must solemnly swear to me that you will not say anything to Sondra about this, and that you will under no circumstances go to see her or otherwise spend time with her alone," Mike said earnestly.

"Of course," Maggie agreed. In the face of her mate's fierceness, she really had no choice. The problem now was figuring out how to keep her promise to Mike and still continue with her own investigation.

She could call Sondra, she decided. That would be a start, now that she knew how Jas fitted in, and had this new information about the probable inaccuracy of the time of death. And she could talk to Kara again. Kara had made a point of telling Maggie where she was all day Sunday, and people who had carefully-thought-out alibis were sometimes suspicious for that very reason. Might she be involved in some way? Maggie hoped not. Kara seemed a troubled but basically good girl. Could Kara be covering for someone else? Her father perhaps? Or Harrison Creitz?

Maggie's musing was interrupted by the ringing of the phone. "Yes, she is, Sondra," she heard Mike say.

She walked over to where he was seated, took the phone from his outstretched hand, and stood at his side to answer.

"Hello, Sondra, I was just thinking of you," she said. "Fine, and you?" She listened for a moment. "I guess so. Sure, I'll be right..." Mike waggled a finger warningly. "Wait, why don't you come down here? Would that be okay?"

When Maggie hung up, she handed the phone back to Mike, who was shaking his head in disbelief. "Well, you said I shouldn't go there," she said, trying to look innocent.

Sondra arrived in just a few minutes, and Maggie whisked her away to the kitchen for tea and talk. The visit to the police station had left Sondra shaken. "They made me go over every fact I had told them," she said, rubbing the smooth porcelain handle of her tea cup with one finger. "And they kept going over and over our...my relationship with Nora through the past five years. I just don't understand what they hoped to gain."

Maggie shook her head sympathetically and took a slow, rather noisy sip of the very hot tea. "Did they ask you about where you were any time that weekend other than Sunday evening?" she asked.

"No, why would they?" Sondra wanted to know.

"Well, I doubt they would, but they should," Maggie said. "It could help eliminate you as a suspect in the long run, if you can tell me where you were on Friday evening and Saturday." She leaned forward, elbows on the table, and looked expectantly at Sondra.

"I could, Maggie, but in this case I don't think I want to," Sondra said, holding her cup in both hands as if to warm her fingers.

"Why not?" Maggie was puzzled.

"I guess I'm just not sure why you want to know," Sondra said, sounding somewhat aloof, "and I don't want people making judgments. I wish you could just respect my boundaries."

"Sondra, how can I help you if you won't cooperate?" Maggie said, exasperated.

"I don't see what it has to do with anything," Sondra said, with a catch in her voice which suggested she was close to tears.

"Sondra, I have good reason to think Nora was killed earlier than the police think—probably on Friday evening, or at the latest, Saturday evening. If I can prove this, then they'll have to look at other possible suspects. But only if you were doing something else Friday evening that can be verified." Maggie was torn between her desire to use whatever persuasions she could to get the information and her anger that Sondra was playing coy.

"If you were somewhere you're ashamed of, I promise I won't tell anyone unless I have to. But you really should tell me, so I know where I stand. Unless you want to go on without my help," Maggie finished up rather crossly.

"I'm not ashamed! It's just...I don't expect you to understand, Maggie. I was with Jas, from early Friday afternoon through all day on Saturday. He came over about 3:00, I suppose, and we never left the house till dinnertime Saturday, when we went out for pizza about 7:30 or 8:00, except I did go to get the paper and the mail.

"You can't know how it is to be approaching middle age alone and have a man of his—well, anyway, that's where I was, and who I was with and I hope you don't have to ask him about, although I don't suppose he'd mind. He says he loves me, which I know he does in his own way, even though he's very young and it will no doubt pass, but it's very nice while it lasts." Sondra looked at Maggie with an expression that seemed in equal parts to plead for understanding and dare criticism.

"Oh, that's all right, Sondra," Maggie said, greatly relieved.

Sondra looked completely nonplused. "That's it? That's all?"

"That's all I needed to know," Maggie said cheerfully. "Was there anything else you needed?"

"Well, I said I came down here to get your help. The police called Sam! Can you believe it?" Sondra paused, her face reddening, and then plunged on. "Can you believe it? And then he called me!"

She paused again, and Maggie took advantage of the space to suggest it wasn't too surprising that Sam would get a call. "But why did he call you?"

"Just to harass me! He assumed I had told them about his affair with Nora!" Sondra continued, speaking more quickly now. "Which of course I did not! I told him half the town knew about it, and the police could have heard it from anyone. Orin, for example. Or even Nora's girls. Augh! The nerve of that man!"

"Well, at least," Maggie said, hoping to calm her down, "at least you were able to assure him you had nothing to do with it. And nothing to do with Nora's death, either. Right?"

"Of course not." Sondra sounded deflated now. She sat staring at her teacup. "I don't think the police believed me either," she said, more to herself than to Maggie.

"Well, I believe you, for whatever that's worth. And once they get the correct time of death, the police will ask for and will have to accept your alibi." Maggie sat back in her chair. "Was there anything else? Can I do anything for you now?"

"I guess not," Sondra said, sounding unsure. "I guess I just needed to see you for a little." She looked sad and a little puzzled, her brows knit together in a tight frown. "I guess that's all. Thanks for the tea, Maggie." She stood up.

Maggie stood up, too. "Oh, one other thing. Did you happen

to see any cars around Nora's house at any time that weekend? I mean, other than Les's when he came to pick her up on Friday?"

"Not that I can think of, but I wouldn't have paid much attention anyway," Sondra said off-handedly.

"Well, give me a hug, my dear," Maggie said, keenly aware that she was keeping a good many secrets. The two embraced, and Maggie walked Sondra to the front door. "Hope to see you soon," Maggie said. "Bye-bye. Do give me a call if you think of anything."

"Bye-bye, see you later, Maggie." Sondra walked down the driveway and disappeared down the street.

Maggie came slowly back into the living room, her mental wheels spinning as she attempted to assimilate the new information.

"Maggie," Mike said, looking up from his armchair, "You need something to take your mind off this murder. Would you like to go for a walk, or take in a movie?"

"Better make it the movie, if it's not too late. I'm going round and round on this business, and I'd probably just talk your ear off about it if we went walking," Maggie said.

"Well, let's do it to it, then," Mike said, rising from his chair. "Do you want a tear-jerker or a comedy?"

They settled for the comedy, which wasn't great but was fast-paced enough to keep Maggie's mind off the murder case. On the way home, they stopped for ice cream, and Mike described to Maggie the current status with the coroner statistics study. As he'd feared, the Director wanted to charge ahead, in spite of the practical and political difficulties.

"He wants me to ask the Legislature for a bill to give us regulatory authority over the coroners, at least over their forms," Mike said, shaking his head sadly. "Fortunately, it's too late in the session for any new bills this year. Maybe by next session, he'll have forgotten about it."

"Do you think Geoff is going to want to go to Wesleyan when he graduates in another year?" Maggie asked on the way home from Baskin-Robbins.

"I don't know. A lot can change in a year, but he sure seemed to be impressed today," Mike said.

"Can we afford for him to go there?" Maggie asked.

"Probably not, unless he gets scholarships like Alyssa," Mike answered. "But they seem to have more scholarships than some places. Not as many as Bethany, but then they aren't as expensive as Bethany is now, either."

Maggie had completed her own B.A. at the same small central Kansas liberal arts college where Alyssa was now majoring in music. Mike, as a newly-hired K.B.I. agent, had been stationed in Lindsborg, the Swedish community which was home to Bethany College. With both children in school, Maggie had started taking classes to supplement her A.A. degree, in addition to working part-time for the local judge. "Are you criticizing my alma mater?" she teased now.

"Just the facts, ma'am, just the facts," Mike lapsed into his Jack Webb imitation.

"I wish I had a little notebook like Sgt. Friday, and people had to answer my questions," Maggie said, yawning. "It would make it much easier for me to figure out this thing with Nora."

"Hey! No more obsessing tonight!" Mike spoke sharply, then softened his tone and continued, "I have better things in mind."

"Please describe in detail what you are thinking of when you say, 'better things,' Mr. Tenwhistle." Maggie cupped her left hand, miming a note-pad, and pretended to be prepared to take notes. But the ensuing conversation soon put all thought of police procedures out of her head, and by the time they arrived home, she was ready for a entirely different kind of activity.

CHAPTER 18

The next day, Sunday, dawned cool and bright. Maggie went outside soon after sunrise, dressed in jeans and a dark blue sweatshirt, with a wool scarf wrapped loosely around her head and neck. She wandered into the back yard, disturbing a pair of cardinals and a flock of sparrows and finches picking up millet spilled from the bird feeders over the winter. "Hi, guys," Maggie said, as much to the trees and bushes as to the birds. She often felt as though this little patch of nature was sentient and responsive to her in a way most places weren't.

She walked over to the small garden patch, where daffodils were pushing themselves through the winter's mulch of fallen leaves. More than a week to bloom, she guessed. Would spring warmth come all at once, as it often did, and then give way quickly to the heat of summer?

She wished she had time to really take care of the yard. Mike wasn't interested in it, and she didn't want him to do the flowers, anyway. It was enough that he and Geoff between them kept the lawn mowed all summer. She pushed idly at the limber branches of forsythia, which looked nearly ready to bloom, and wondered what it would be like when Geoff, too, moved away. Maybe once they got both kids out of school, either she or Mike could go back, get an advanced degree. First, though, she'd better learn what she could about the brokerage business, and get that license.

Shivering slightly against the wind, Maggie walked back through the carport into the front drive to pick up the papers. She and Mike made a ritual of reading the Sunday papers together, with reading the good bits aloud permitted for everything but the comics. She went back inside and started the coffee.

After the papers, and breakfast, and another walk around the yard, Maggie could no longer hold off thinking about "the case," even if Mike thought she should leave it to the pros. She sat down at the kitchen table and made two lists, headed respectively "Things I Know" and "Things I Don't Know." Next to the "Things I Know," she wrote corresponding "Implications Thereof." Next to "Things I Don't Know," she wrote "How I Could Find Out," a column which had a lot of items that began "Ask" and ended with a name. When the latter list began to show a regular pattern of three names, Maggie decided to do some telephoning.

First, she called Kara Patterson. Then she called Orin. Finally, she called Leslie Stone. "Hello, Leslie?" Maggie said, trying to keep her voice absolutely neutral.

"Yes," Les answered.

"I was wondering whether you were going to be coming to town any time today. Were you coming to the co-op work day or anything?"

"Uh, yes, as a matter of fact, I, uh, had planned to come in a little later. Uh, why?" Les replied.

"Well, I was wanting to talk to you. I've been reading about the workshops Baba Sin De gives, and I got to wondering about the diet Nora was on, and what you have been doing. I think I've found out something about Nora's diet that might be of interest to you." Maggie stopped, afraid she would scare him off.

"Oh, uh, yes, well, we could meet at the co-op. Uh, at about three?" Les phrased it as a question.

"That's fine," Maggie said. "We could maybe sit and talk out on the loading dock. Okay, well, see you then. Bye-bye."

"Bye-bye."

Maggie heard the click of Les's phone hanging up and breathed a sigh of relief as she too hung up.

"Mike, I'm going to go see Kara Patterson," she told her husband.

"Okay, Tiger. Be careful," Mike said, looking up from his arm chair, where he had started another mystery novel. "Will you be back for lunch?"

"Yup, for sure," Maggie said lightly. "I shouldn't be long."

On the way to Kara's apartment, Maggie considered how to approach what she needed to ask Kara. She probably would need all the leverage she could command (or invent) in order to get the truth, which she was quite sure she hadn't gotten yet.

The apartment was in a large complex, not far from the Washburn campus. Maggie parked in one of the few empty stalls marked "VISITOR," and located the correct building and door number. Kara opened the door promptly in response to Maggie's ring. She seemed very slight, wearing purple stretch pants and a dark gold sweatshirt. "Hello, Mrs. Tenwhistle," she said, smiling and holding the door aside.

"I'd be glad if you'd call me "Maggie," Maggie said. "'Mrs. Tenwhistle' sounds like my mother-in-law." She laughed softly to show it was meant as a joke.

"Okay, Maggie," Kara said. "Please make yourself at home." She indicated the very-much-used looking couch slipcovered in faded striped denim, and the single overstuffed chair of similar vintage and condition. "Typical student apartment, I'm afraid, but it's home. Can I get you something to drink? Diet cola, or some coffee?"

"Maybe a glass of water, if it's easy," Maggie said. "I don't need ice." She sat carefully on the couch. It was lumpy, but she felt no springs poking through.

Kara got the water, and brought it to Maggie. For herself, she popped the top of a can of Diet Coke. "You said you needed to talk to me about my mother?"

"Uh-huh," Maggie murmured, and took a sip of the water. "I've been thinking a lot about what you and I talked about on

Friday, and if you don't mind, before I tell you what I have come up with, I'd like to ask you a few questions."

"Okay," Kara agreed. "Of course, the police asked me lots and lots of questions, right after Mother died. But I guess it's okay. Go ahead."

"You said you were with friends on Sunday, during the day, and with your dad on Sunday night. Can you tell me where you were the rest of the weekend? What did you do Friday after you left your mother, for instance?" Maggie tried to arrange her face to look as though this were the most natural question in the world to be asking.

"I was so angry with Mother, I went over to Dad and Lorraine's and crashed in my old room. I must have slept for three hours, until 9:00 or so. Then I woke up and went home and slept all night, too." Kara shook her head at the memory.

"Did you tell your dad and stepmother about the fight with your mother?" Maggie asked, keeping her voice as casual as possible.

"When I came bursting in on them, I must have said something. Probably I was swearing! I don't really remember. I'm sure Dad asked what was wrong, and I'm sure I said something vague. I didn't tell him what the fight was over, of course," Kara looked at Maggie with new interest. "I don't think Lorraine stayed around to hear any of whatever I did say. She usually leaves when I've got personal stuff to discuss with Dad."

"And then you went to sleep, and slept all evening, and then went home." Maggie thought a moment, and then asked, "So what did you do on Saturday?"

"Saturday, I—I don't understand what sense any of this makes. What difference does it make where I was on Saturday?" Kara asked. She took a sip of soda and looked appraisingly at Maggie.

"If you can, just bear with me for another minute or two," Maggie begged. "I will tell you, but I want to get these questions out of the way first."

"Well, Saturday, I think I spent most of the day in the

library. I know I went to a basketball tournament game that night, with some girlfriends." Kara tapped her Coke can with her fingertips.

"Did you see your father at all on Saturday?" Maggie asked, knowing she was pushing her luck.

"No," Kara replied. "But what does that have to do with anything?"

"Kara, I'm pretty sure whoever killed your mother must have put her body in the freezer to disguise the time of her death. And then they came back, took her body out of the freezer, and let themselves out of the house somehow, leaving all the doors locked, to make it look like suicide."

"Let themselves out of the house? But how? The police found Mother's keys in the house."

"Through the garage?"

"But it was closed up…oh, God! It couldn't be!"

"What, Kara? You'd better tell me."

"My garage door opener. It was at my dad's on Sunday night. He said I must have left it there Friday night. I couldn't understand how it got out of my car. I never take it out. But if my dad…Mrs. Ten—Maggie, you don't think my dad could have…" Kara stood up and began to pace the small living room.

"I don't think he could have. Of course, I was asleep, but still—he wouldn't, he couldn't!" she said, talking more to herself than to Maggie. "No," she said, turning to face Maggie, "I don't think that could possibly be right."

"Well, maybe there is some other explanation," Maggie said. "And you can be sure I will be trying to find it. There is one other thing you could answer for me. When you were with your mother Friday night, did she say anything to make you think she was expecting a visitor? Or that she was planning to go somewhere? Anything that would suggest there was someone coming after you left?"

"No, I don't think so. I wasn't there very long, but—no, I'm pretty sure not. If you'd asked me at the time, I'd have said she was scheduled to go to K.C. that night. But now—I think she was wearing some kind of robe, so I would assume she was in for the night." Kara sat down again, curling her feet under her. She looked like a small child, lonely and afraid.

Maggie stood up. "Kara, I think better go now."

"Mrs. Tenwhistle, there's one more thing," Kara said miserably. "We washed out the freezer at Mom's house yesterday, after we unplugged it." She looked up at Maggie with pain on her beautiful young face. "My father insisted on it."

"Is there a friend you can call to come stay with you?" Maggie asked, concerned. Kara nodded. "Will you call her as soon as I leave?" She nodded again, more forcefully.

Maggie moved toward the door. "Please don't say anything to anyone, not anyone, about this conversation. It could be dangerous for you. Someone has been very determined to leave no loose ends, and if that someone should get the idea that things are beginning to unravel—well, there's already been one murder."

"But you can't think my father…" Kara's voice rose and then trailed off.

"I don't know," Maggie said. "But I'm going to find out!"

CHAPTER 19

Back home, Maggie busied herself with fixing lunch. Geoff was sitting in the living room with his dad, where they were arguing about politics, or so Maggie gathered from the tone of their discussion. Leaving cheese sandwiches heating slowly in her largest skillet, Maggie walked in to join her family.

"Hi, Mom," Geoff said, breaking off an exposition of the stupidity of the current administration.

"Hi, wooly," Maggie said, tousling his uncombed hair affectionately. "Are you guys getting all the problems of the world solved?"

"Real close," Mike said. "Are you ready for lunch?"

"Just about. If someone would come set the table, and someone else make a green salad, we'd be there."

After lunch, Geoff offered to do the dishes. "Something wrong with the kid?" Mike queried after he and Maggie had adjourned to the living room.

"Don't make fun of him, Mike," Maggie scolded. "He's a good boy."

"I know he is," Mike said, giving his wife a gentle pat on the buns.

"And what are your plans for the afternoon?" Maggie asked. "Going to play some golf?"

"I don't think so," Mike said. "At least, not till later, if at all. It'll be crowded as heck out there now. No, I thought I might go to the library and take some books back. Want to come along?"

"No, I think not," Maggie said, mentally crossing her

fingers behind her back. "I have some things I want to get done." It wasn't a lie, she told herself, just a truth told with intent to deceive. "Are you going right now?"

"I guess so. Then if I feel like trying a little golf later, I won't have to rush." Mike began gathering up library books. "Do you have any you need returned?" he asked.

"Not this time, thanks. Well, have fun!" Maggie kissed him lightly on the cheek as he bent down to pick up a book from the floor beside his chair.

"You too," he said. "Bye, Tiger."

Maggie strolled out into the kitchen where Geoff was finishing the dishes. "Here, let me hand you this pan from the stove," Maggie said. "And here are a couple of cups you missed."

"Great, Mom," Geoff grumbled. "I was just letting the water out."

"Well, at least put the pan to soak, will you?" Maggie sighed. You just can't get good help these days, she thought but didn't say.

"Sure, Mom," Geoff said cheerfully, running water into the skillet. "Well, I'm off. See you tonight. I may be late."

"How late is late? Tomorrow is a school day," Maggie cautioned.

"Oh, ten, ten-thirty, probably. No later than 11:00," Geoff hedged.

"Better make it no later than 10:30, if you please. It really does disturb my sleep when you come in at 11:00 or 11:30. I have trouble getting back to sleep. Okay?" Maggie looked up at her son, who was almost as tall as his father.

"Okay, Mom, I'll do my best." Geoff slid around his mother and bounced up the stairs. A moment later, he was back at the front door, CD player in hand. "Bye, Mom."

"Goodbye, Son, drive carefully." Maggie checked her watch. She had half an hour before her next appointment.

She had just begun gathering up newspapers in the living room when the phone rang. Following the sound, she found the phone where it belonged, on the side table, but hidden under the

"Parade" magazine Mike had been reading. "Hello," she said into the mouthpiece.

At first she heard nothing in reply. "Hello," she said again.

She heard an intake of breath, and then a muffled voice began to speak in exaggerated rhythm:

"Maggie the Cat, super snoop,
Wants to gather all the poop.
Tries to find the secret clue.

Not so wise a thing to do.
Curiosity killed the Cat,
And my, oh, my, we don't want that!
So Maggie, careful where you go;
You could join Nora down below!"

Maggie was too surprised to speak at first. "What?" she said. "Who is this? This isn't funny, whoever you are."

The line went dead, and Maggie nearly dropped the phone. She was beginning to tremble as she dropped heavily into Mike's chair and fumbled to hang up the receiver. Her breath was coming in loud, shaky gasps.

Slow, even inhales, loud exhales, she told herself. Now, slowly, slowly, breathe. She began to get control rather quickly, as her mind raced to make sense of what had just happened. Was it someone's idea of a practical joke? Not Mike—he wouldn't ever find murder funny, and he certainly didn't think Maggie's involvement was to be joked about. And not Geoff. So far as Maggie knew, he wasn't really aware of what she was doing, and besides, a cruel joke was not at all his style, either.

Was it even a man? Maggie thought so, but she couldn't be sure. The voice was muffled, and could have been pitched much differently than the usual speech of the caller. Certainly it wasn't recognizable. So it could have been one of her friends, but again —not their style.

That left people involved with Nora's death, who knew Maggie was "curious." The Friedmanns? Highly unlikely. What could prompt Helda or Buff to do such a hurtful thing?

Kara? Again Maggie doubted it. One of the young men? Possible, but only if Kara or Sondra had talked with them about Maggie's investigation. Sondra, yes, possible, but that would mean she was involved in the crime somehow. The other two possibilities were the two men Maggie was planning to visit in the next two hours. Should she cancel her plans? But that would be to let the threat do what its author no doubt wanted—to scare her off. He (or, less likely, she) would find Maggie the Cat didn't scare so easily.

Maggie started to rise, and sat down again abruptly. Her legs were like Gumby's. She took a deep breath, closed her eyes, and concentrated her attention to the soles of her feet. Connected to the earth. Opening to the clear, strong flowing energy of the Mother Earth herself, roots going deep into the soil, past the bedrock, to the fiery, strong center of the planet. Flowing back up to strengthen and energize, protect, and catalyze. She held the image for several long deep breaths, and then opened her eyes and stood slowly. Much better.

Maggie looked at the clock. Time to get ready to go see Orin Patterson. She climbed the stairs, taking them slow and easy but noticing that she felt pretty solid. She stopped to brush her hair, and slipped on a pair of quartz crystal pendant earring. So what if they didn't go with sweats?

Maggie wrote a note to Mike, and then carefully checked her bag for keys before locking the door. Inside the car, she took a couple of extra minutes to visualize a silver egg of protection around herself, her car, her house, and Mike, Alyssa, Geoff, wherever each of them was. "Thank you, Mother-Father," she breathed. "So may it be."

Orin and Lorraine Patterson lived in a large attractive one-story brick home uphill from the country club. The lawn swept gracefully from the curb, with artistically-placed shrubs and trees drawing the eye in a pleasing line. Orin had agreed to meet with Maggie surprisingly quickly. Maggie wasn't quite sure what to make of his eagerness to cooperate. Well, she'd soon see.

Inside, the house was equally attractive. Lorraine, who had come to the door, escorted Maggie into the living room, a large L-shaped room with a limestone fireplace, thick light rosy-brown carpet, and comfortable, substantial furniture. Orin stood when Maggie and Lorraine entered and strode toward them. "Come in, Maggie. How nice to see you!" He stretched out a well-manicured hand, and shook hers warmly.

Lorraine said softly, "Nice to see you, Maggie. I'll let you and Orin have your talk." Before Maggie could reply, the second Mrs. Patterson had turned and left the room.

"Won't you sit down?" Orin gestured to one of the soft chairs by a coffee table near the large picture window. "Can I get you something? Some coffee, or a drink?" He gestured toward a well-stocked bar, complete with an insulated carafe which Maggie assumed contained coffee.

"No, thanks, but you go ahead," Maggie said. She didn't need any further stimulation, and she certainly didn't want any alcohol.

"I will, if you'll excuse me. Are you sure I can't pour something for you? I have soft drinks." Orin poured himself a small glass from what Maggie guessed was a bottle of sherry.

"No, thanks, really. I'm fine," she said. "You have a lovely home."

"Thank you. Lorraine is an artist, and she loves her house." Orin smiled, carrying his drink back to a chair near Maggie. "This has been a difficult week, for me at least. To happier times ahead." He saluted Maggie with the glass and drank a sip. "So, what do you have for me?"

He's used to being the one in charge, Maggie thought. This is his territory, and he's an experienced interviewer, a professional negotiator. Watch your step, Maggie girl. "I talked to Kara this morning," she said, watching his face carefully. "I told her I knew her mother wasn't killed on Sunday night as the coroner originally said. Kara had already told me about the fight she and Nora had on Friday evening." Orin's face did not change, though Maggie noticed he was gripping the delicate sherry glass more tightly than caution might have dictated. "Do you know what the fight was about, Orin?" Maggie asked.

"Suppose you tell me," he parried.

"Nora had seduced young Harrison Creitz, whom Kara had been dating for some time. The man who sang at the funeral this week. When Kara found out about it, she went over to 'have it out' with her mother—her words, not mine. She's a feisty young woman, your daughter," Maggie said, trying to put a objectivity she did not feel into her words.

"She would be an obvious suspect, if it were not for the time of death being set as Sunday evening, when Kara was with you and Lorraine. She had access to the house, both a key and an electronic garage door opener. She certainly had strong motive. She admits she hated her mother, for what she had done to you and the whole family, as well as for this latest insult. And who would be more likely to know where the gun was kept? Nora's house had been Kara's home, too, after all, until just last year.

"So the alibi for the time of death is very, very important. That's too bad, because I think Kara is as innocent as she says she is. But when the police finish checking out the effects a number of hours in a freezer would have on a time of death calculation, it will look very likely that Nora was murdered not Sunday night, but Saturday night, or even more likely Friday night, just about the time Kara was there."

"Why would the police check out a hair-brained theory like that?" Orin cleared his throat.

"Maybe they will notice the stack of plastic cartons full of fruits and nuts that are half-hidden in Nora's compost bin. Or maybe the lab will turn up something. Even if you have had time to clean out the inside of the freezer, which Kara told me you insisted on doing, there may still be traces of hair or blood or skin caught in a crevice. Or maybe you have thrown away but not burned the rags and sponges you used to clean it with." (Maggie thought she saw a shadow of dismay cross his face on that one.)

"And I have the turtle, which was in the freezer after Nora's body was there. You were right, saving it back was vital—Sondra was sure to ask for it—but it now may have traces of something incriminating on it. Or, perhaps Kara will tell the police what she told me. Because I've already told them about the freezer." (What would my father say if he could hear me lying like this with a perfectly straight face? Maggie wondered irrelevantly.)

Orin's shoulders slumped and his handsome face took on a look of defeat that was painful to see. "I didn't expect her to be dead!" he said. "Kara came over here so upset. She didn't say much, but I understood her mother had done something really outrageous this time. When Kara fell asleep on the sofa I went over to Nora's, ready to—I don't know what—but I wasn't prepared to see her dead. The front door was unlocked, and when she didn't answer, I walked in, and there she was.

"I felt sure the shooting must have been an accident. Kara isn't capable of cold-blooded murder. But I also knew she was bound to be suspected. It seemed a simple enough thing to do, to clear out the freezer and put Nora's body in. She was light as a feather, just skin and bones—from that crazy diet, I suppose." Orin spoke slowly but evenly, without much expression. "There wasn't even much blood. Her robe was falling off; I wrapped her in a blanket.

"Then there was the problem of what to do with all that frozen food," he continued. "I couldn't leave it to melt there on the kitchen floor, so I put it in two trash bags and hauled them out to the compost bin. Nora had raked up a great pile of leaves just beside the bin, so after I put the food in, I covered it up as best I could with the leaves. It seemed fairly safe."

Orin paused and held his hands out in front of him, slowly knitting and un-knitting his outspread fingers. "I wiped off the gun, just in case it had Kara's fingerprints on it, and left the house closed up, taking Nora's keys. When I got back to my house, I took Kara's garage door opener out of her car, figuring that would make it easier to leave the house completely locked up afterward. I wasn't worried about Kara missing her opener to Nora's garage, since she knew her mother was leaving for Kansas City. I hoped the death would be ruled a suicide, but if not, at least the time of death would be thrown off far enough to confuse everything."

As Maggie watched, Orin Patterson seemed to be shrinking before her eyes. He hunched forward in his chair, and released a heavy sigh. "Then Sunday afternoon, I slipped out while Lorraine thought I was napping and took Nora, her body, that is, out of the freezer, put the robe back on, and put her back in the chair. I'd had to bend her into a sitting position to get her in the freezer, so that's the way…I had to hurry. I couldn't risk Lorraine missing me or someone seeing me coming or going. Of course, I parked down the street, but still there was always that chance, and the longer I stayed, the greater the danger of exposure. Then I got back home, and when I had the opportunity I returned Kara's garage door opener to her. The rest you know."

"You made sure you, Kara, and Lorraine had alibis for as much of the weekend as possible," Maggie said, "in hopes of covering whatever time the coroner would set as the time of death. As it turned out, he picked the time you were all three at home together, so it couldn't have been better. Were you prepared to lie to the police to establish an alibi if necessary?" she asked.

"Of course, if necessary to protect my daughter," Orin said with a straightforward conviction that Maggie couldn't help admiring.

"Tell me," Maggie asked, "that day of the flood at Sondra's, when we took the carpet out?"

"I was afraid you were going to check out the compost pile," Orin completed her sentence. He straightened a bit. "So I made up something to distract your attention. I didn't count on your remembering it and going back later." He sighed again and stared at his hands.

"Orin," Maggie said, "Orin, look at me." He looked up

slowly. "Orin, I believe you, and I think the police will too. You are going to be in trouble for obstructing the investigation, of course." In fact, Maggie added mentally, you could very likely lose your ticket to practice law.

"But," she continued aloud, "it will be much better for you if you go to see them instead of waiting for them to come for you.

"I'm going to leave now, but I'd feel much better if I knew you were going to get Lorraine and go down to the station right now and give them your story." Maggie paused. Orin was staring at her as though hanging on her every word. "Will you do that, Orin?"

He nodded. "Yes, I believe I will. Thank you, Maggie."

"Don't thank me yet. I have one more interview today," Maggie said. "And I need to go get ready for it."

CHAPTER 20

By 2:55, Maggie was kicking her heels against the concrete loading dock in the alley behind the co-op. She stared at the back doors of the small apartments across the alley. Little windows, all of them with curtains or blinds closed. No indications anywhere that the back entrances were in frequent use. No traffic up and down the alley. Quite a lonely place, actually.

She hoped to intercept Les before he went into the store, so she was trying to watch the small parking lot at the side of the building. A large pine tree partially blocked her view, however, and she wondered whether she might already have missed seeing him come. If she didn't see him drive up in a few minutes, she'd have to go into the co-op and look for him there.

But she did see him drive up, the little engine of his old orange VW purring smoothly. She called to him as he was getting out of the car, and waved gaily. "Hi, Les, over here." She mustn't overdo the Miss Congeniality bit, she supposed.

Les walked over to the five foot high dock. He started to lean his back against it and then bent his elbows and, placing his hands palm down on top of the dock, hoisted himself straight up to sit beside Maggie. Strong, she thought.

"Hi, Maggie. Nice to see you," he said.

"How are you doing, Les?" Maggie inquired.

"Oh, I'm, uh, just fine," Les said. "And you?"

"Actually, I've been better. Things have been a bit tense for me lately. That's why I wanted to talk to you," Maggie replied.

"I'm, uh, sorry to hear that," Les said. "How can I, uh, be of help?" His herringbone-striped overalls showed a lot of wear and were patched on one thigh with a neat square of red bandanna. His ropey, muscular arms and large bony hands seemed well suited to a farmer, which he had at one time been, or a carpenter, which he currently was.

"Les, can you tell me what Nora's special diet was, and why she was on it? And while you're at it, tell me the same things about yours, how it differs from Nora's and what you feel you get out of it."

"As far as I know, uh, Nora was eating, oh, uh, fruits and, you know, well, uh, nuts, and nothing more. Baba felt she was ready for such a diet. Baba takes only, uh, a little fruit juice himself, and, uh, most of his nutrients he, uh, oh, he gets from the air, you know."

Maggie didn't know, but she also didn't want to get distracted into a discussion of breatharian philosophy. "And you, Les, what is your diet? If you don't mind talking about it."

Les hesitated for a moment, as though thinking that through. "No," he said finally, "I don't mind. I was, oh, well, strictly brown rice and clear water, for about six months. I found this salutary. But Baba said I was being too, uh, well, too harsh—well, perhaps not too harsh, but, uh, oh, glorying in the hardship instead of using it for, uh, purification.'

"So?" Maggie prompted.

"So I've been adding some vegetables, and, uh—I think I told you this, uh, just not long ago."

"Les, why didn't you tell me Nora did not go to Kansas City with you last weekend?" There was now no turning back. Unless Les had a plausible explanation, Maggie would have to go all the way. She hoped she was right in assuming he would stay rational. Having chosen this spot as private enough for conversation but public enough for safety, she would soon discover whether she'd planned adequately. The industrial-sized dumpster below the dock seemed to loom threateningly as she waited for Les to speak.

"What, uh, what do you mean?" Les sounded surprised.

"Les, I talked to Kathy Gegeshina. She told me Nora never

showed up, that you came alone." From the side, Maggie watched his face, slightly upturned into the sun, so that his eyes were squinted almost closed against the light.

"Uh, I, uh, you didn't ask, that is, you didn't ask me, uh, whether she went. It, uh, it didn't come up. That's all," he said finally. His tight smile told Maggie nothing.

"I think it was more than that. I think you didn't want me to know because of something that happened between you and Nora before you left for Kansas City. Les, look at me, please," she commanded rather than pled.

He turned toward her and opened his eyes, blinking furiously and flexing his strong hands.

"Les," she said softly, "I know that Nora was not killed on Sunday evening. I know she was killed on Friday, before you left to drive to Kansas City. Sondra saw you drive up to Nora's house —and no one has seen Nora alive since you left." Maggie couldn't entirely control an involuntary shudder.

But Les didn't see it. He had turned his face upward again, and closed his eyes. He gave no sign of listening to Maggie.

"Orin Patterson found the body—it must have been minutes after you left, Les. It won't take the police long to track down when you were there, or to establish just when Nora died, given the new evidence from Sondra and Orin." Maggie was by no means as sure as she was trying to sound.

"Orin has gone to the police already," I hope, she thought. "And now that they know what they're looking for, they will find physical evidence of your having been in the house." None of this was likely, but Maggie hoped Les wouldn't realize it—or wouldn't care.

Les continued to stare at the sun from behind closed eyelids. When he spoke, it was in a voice Maggie had never heard before, rich and vibrant, with no trace of the hesitancy he usually displayed. "I didn't mean to kill her," he said. "Not at first. I went to pick her up to drive to Kansas City.

"She wasn't ready to go. She was only partially clothed!

She invited me to—she's a very attractive woman, you know." Les turned and looked directly at Maggie, eyes meeting hers, as though asking for confirmation. Maggie nodded, afraid of breaking the spell.

"She used sex as entertainment, and men were her playthings. She said it was part of her path to enlightenment, but Baba was wrong about her. She wasn't interested in enlightenment. She'd tease a man, sounding all so innocent and spiritual, talking about how much the world needs love. All the while her body and her eyes were saying what kind of love she was really interested in.

"I'm a man. I have a man's desires, a man's appetites. Only by denying appetite, by bringing the body under the control of the will can a man progress. She was trying to lure me from my path. Maybe it was a challenge to her, but it would have destroyed me. I couldn't let it happen again.

"Baba says it is good for us to be tested, but woe to her by whom the temptation comes. I told her 'No.' I tried to leave. She rubbed herself against me. She—" For a moment, Les seemed lost in recollection. Maggie held her breath.

Les breathed deeply, and Maggie breathed with him, willing him to continue. "When I pushed her away, she pulled a gun out of a drawer and handed it to me. She taunted me, saying if I was really dedicated, I should rid myself of my temptation. She stood there, displaying herself openly, still saying those terrible things, and daring me to shoot her, if it was the only way I could resist her.

"It was blasphemous, the way she talked. She had no right to talk to me that way. She laughed at me, called me a pitiful excuse for a man. She had no right. I couldn't take it any more." Les closed his eyes again.

"So you shot her," Maggie said, making it a statement, not a question. Les nodded. "And then what?"

"It was so loud," Les said. His voice rose and took on the hesitant, whiny quality that was its more usual tone. "I, uh, dropped the gun and, uh, you know, left the house. I got in my car and drove to Kansas City. When I came home, I expected, oh, uh, to be arrested, you know. When I wasn't, I, uh, hoped it had all been, uh, just a nightmare. When, uh, oh, you seemed to be suspicious of me, and no one else was, I, uh, hoped I could warn you off. I didn't want to have killed her."

CHAPTER 21

"And then Mike drove up, and after him, Carl Nelson in a patrol car with a couple of uniformed officers," Maggie told the Tuesday night group a few days later. "Mike had figured out what I was up to, from the note I'd left, and called Carl. Orin had just showed up at the station, and Carl was on his way down there, so he and Mike put two and two together and came rushing over to rescue me!"

"The knights on their chargers!" Laurie sniffed.

"Actually, I was glad to see them. I hadn't thought out what came next, and I don't know what I would have done if Les had decided to stonewall. But he didn't. I think he was actually relieved to be able to tell his story. He had been living with this for almost ten days, and the tension must have been nearly unbearable."

"He'll be under psychiatric observation, no doubt," Anna said.

"I'm sure he will," Maggie said. "I can't vouch for whether he'll be found able to stand trial, but if he is, a verdict of temporary insanity wouldn't surprise me."

"I wonder what could have brought him to such a state?" Anna mused. "His mother died a while ago, I think, out there in Auburn, some time after they lost the farm."

"But that was over a year ago that his mother died," Laurie said. "I'd wondered about a chemical imbalance, maybe from so many months on that extreme diet of his."

"Mike would love hearing it was that," Maggie laughed wryly.

"Are you going to have him charged with the break-in and the threatening call?" Suz wanted to know.

"I don't think so," Maggie said. "It's up to Mike, but my thought is: one, he didn't really break in, he only unlocked the door with my hidden key, and two, the phone call was made out of desperation and didn't really scare me that much anyway. I'm much more interested in his getting help than I am in prosecuting him for those little things.

"Now Mike may have a different idea. He certainly has some ideas about the front door! He's been saying for years that we have to get a dead bolt lock that locks and unlocks outside only with a key. I've always said we couldn't afford to replace the old door and what's the point of a dead bolt if you have a hollow core door that any petty burglar could smash through in a minute. So now we are going to get a new door, with a dead bolt, whether we can afford it or not!"

When the news first broke of Leslie's arrest, the Topeka P.D. gave credit to "an unnamed citizen who came forward with information leading to the closure of the case." But in less than twenty-four hours word leaked to the press that the unnamed citizen was Maggie Tenwhistle, wife of K.B.I. Assistant Director Joseph Tenwhistle. Alyssa, having heard the story on the radio, called from college to congratulate her mother, and Geoff came home from school with a dime store sheriff's badge which he ceremoniously pinned on his mother's chest.

At the offices of Blain, Towneshend, and Hannigan, Terence was delighted and asked Maggie endless questions about the case. Constance was appalled: "You might have been in terrible danger, Maggie," she said. Nelson was merely perplexed; he professed not to understand how mere personal emotions could lead one human being to murder another.

Helda Friedmann called Maggie to add her own and her husband's congratulations. "Buff says to tell you he would welcome an opportunity to visit with you about the case at your convenience," she told Maggie. "He finds the possible psychological ramifications quite fascinating."

Public and press were incensed to learn the coroner had missed the fact that the body had been "on ice," thus skewing the estimate of time of death. "Asked to explain why changes in body tissue due to the chilling of the body were not picked up during the forensic investigation, Coroner Albert Williams had no immediate comment," the KSNT Evening News anchor reported Monday night. By the next evening, he was reporting that "in the wake of recent charges of fiscal and personnel mismanagement by Coroner Albert Williams and last week's alleged bungling by his department of the autopsy in a homicide, County Council members today were calling for an investigation of Williams and his department."

On Wednesday evening, Sondra came by. "I guess I didn't really take the whole thing seriously," she admitted. "I do thank you for what you did, Maggie, especially since I wasn't much help."

Maggie mumbled something about curiosity and a drive to find out the truth. She wasn't sure what her motivation had been; her actions of the past several days seemed, even to herself, quite unlike her usual behavior.

"And she took the turtle!" Maggie told Mike at bedtime that night. "She's decided that the 'bad vibes' were nothing to do with Yertle, but had to do with his having been in the freezer with Nora. So she was willing to have him back at her house until the girls come home in May."

"Well, that's one good thing out of this whole mess," Mike said. After he finished being alarmed by the thought of the danger Maggie had exposed herself to, Mike was embarrassed by the publicity and more than a little angry with Maggie. He stomped around the house for a whole evening muttering that he hadn't married a woman private eye, and there wasn't room for two detectives in the house.

But he got over it, of course, and, of course, it didn't take more than a few days for the latest housing authority scandal to chase any lingering interest in the case from the attention of the press and public.

THE END

ACKNOWLEDGEMENTS

Heartfelt thanks to all the friends who have made this effort so enjoyable. Among them, first readers and always my best encouragers, Lynn and Jay; other early readers, some who liked it and some who didn't, including Jim, Elisabeth, and Mary; proofreaders extraordinaire Rhoda and Mike; and all the readers who kept asking when the next book will be out. I'm sure I have left off some names--please forgive, and know I thank you, too.

ABOUT THE AUTHOR

M. J. Van Buren

M. J. Van Buren has lived most of her adult life around the edges of the Flint Hills, with intermittent sojourns in more exotic places such as Brooklyn, New York, and Auckland, New Zealand. She now lives in Topeka, Kansas, with her husband and rather too many houseplants.

BOOKS BY THIS AUTHOR

In Our Hands: An Energy Adventure For The Slightly Skeptical

In Our Hands is a non-fiction account of the author's explorations of the subtle energy of special places and living beings. Published by Carlsons' Publishing, 1997. Available from the author.

Dark Moon Over Brooklyn

 When retired psychology professor Kitty Toulkes opened the door of her Brooklyn apartment one early morning, she had no idea she was opening her life to both deadly danger and a passionate love affair. But in a few short days, she found herself taking part in a Wiccan ceremony, getting up close and way too personal with a creepy masher, and receiving an offer she couldn't refuse from a persistent government agent.